Wolf
Mother

RICHARD COLLIS

Published in 2024 by Discover Your Bounce Publishing

www.discoveryourbouncepublishing.com

978-1-914428-31-9

This is a work of fiction. Names, characters, businesses, places, events, locales, and incidents are either the products of the author's imagination or used in a fictitious manner. Any resemblance to actual persons, living or dead, or actual events is purely coincidental.

Page design and typesetting by Discover Your Bounce Publishing.

PRAISE FOR THE POOL

"Wonderfully paced and evocative use of language make this one of my favourite novels of recent times."

"The world of Fenwood is richly realised in this exciting, fantasy adventure. The upturn of pace that kicks in as the story unfolds is exciting and darker than expected (in a very good way!). I couldn't put it down."

"Collis' storytelling is a masterclass in atmosphere and ambiance."

"Richard is a natural story-teller."

"A captivating and well paced story that draws you in with its richly described settings and characters."

Wolf Mother is the second of the Fenwood tales, set before the events of The Pool.

My darling child,

I begin to understand that my fate is to carry you and give life to you, but for Nature to raise you as its own. The violence I have faced has been my test to prove my strength, my power, my love.

You will be a healer, a warrior, justice and vengeance. You who are born from the vessel of Nature. You who have been touched by fire, awakened by howls, baptised in tears and cradled by the earth. You who are peace and chaos. You who will be loved and hunted.

You are life.
    You are change.
    You are my blood.

I love you.

Mother.

CHAPTER ONE
THEN

The baying crowd smelled blood. They shoved and bared their teeth and howled their way along the churned, cobbled route to the village square. On either side of the track, wooden-framed houses rose up over the procession, where more and more people hung from windows yelling and growling at the prisoners and their vengeful followers. The large cart wheels lumbered on over the uneven stones, leading the bloodthirsty villagers in a demonic parade. Three defeated women, chained miserably to the cage on the deck of the cart, dripped with muddy river water, eyes to the floor and ears closed to the vicious words and accusations stabbing in their direction. Their words meandered their way like a crimson river down the city streets, flowing around the corners, crashing against the banks of people who lined the roadside, spurring on the rocking wagon with wild expressions of fury.

At last, the grotesque procession reached its ghastly final stop. A bonfire raged fiercely on the stone dais at the centre of the square, lascivious tendrils of flame curling out towards the gathering mob. Something in the realisation of what was happening quelled the crowd. The rickety cart squeaked to a halt on the flagstones. A hush descended. The expectant crowd jostled for position and looked toward the southern end of the town square where the mobile prison now halted. Ominously, a hooded figure stepped onto a platform at the back of the cart and, keys jangling, unlocked the cage door. Taking the chain in his grubby hands, one sharp tug brought all three haggard women to their feet and lurching toward the open wood-crossed door. Descending the steps to the dusty, paved floor, the chains around their midriffs clanked in the deafening silence of the crowd, broken only by the crackling of the fire, a violent background melody. Nobody spoke, perhaps afraid that they might incite some incantation from one of these wretched, damned souls. The first two figures held their glassy gaze fixed downwards. Not the third. She looked furtively from side to side, green eyes desperate beneath lank, black hair.

"Please," she whispered, "please…"

No one met her eye. No one responded to her anguish. Her focus fell instead on the inferno ahead, the heat of which was already pricking her skin at some distance. She gasped. In front of the doomed trio, the expectant horde parted, forming an aisle to the burning heart of the chaotic ritual. Clasping her bony fingers together, she closed her tear-filled eyes and muttered a prayer to her Gods.

And then it happened.

A rogue spark. A single flaming fragment. A dancing ember. Drifting, floating, settling in a pocket of the throng. Straw, unseen and insignificant, ignited. The cloth kindling of a peasant's shoe. A ragged cry of sudden awareness. Flailing leg, fanning the flames. Horror. Hot, red destruction leaping between easy targets in a confined space. Pushing. Turmoil. The crowd surged and scattered. Chaos. Frantic. Panic. The paved square erupting into a glowing, burning vision of hatred. Skirt tails and shirt cuffs fell prey to the flicking tongues of flame. Cloths, silks, hessian erupting. The roaring sound of fiery rage became one with the guttural screams of pain, a hellish harmony that bounced off the surrounding walls of buildings that began to be lost in smoke. A stench of burning flesh drifted to the skies with the black clouds, filled with spitting fire and grotesque ash. An engulfed figure careering into the prison cart; the hooded man, now a white shadow in fire.

The chain wrapped about the prisoner's frail waist suddenly felt looser without the forceful hands tugging and twisting it. Somehow, in the midst of the hell around her, pragmatism struck her like a cold force. The third prisoner forced the heating metal links down over her slender hips and let them clatter to the ground. Next to her, the buxom convict looked down at her own motherly hips and back up into the eyes of her now free compatriot. Flames licked at their reddening skin.

"Help me," she hissed. Looking for compassion in the eyes of the raven-haired woman, she saw only the reflection of the flames. "Help me!" she cried, panic reverberating in her tone. The smaller-framed figure began to back away. A strangled cry of desperation escaped the throat of the heavy-set woman who tried to edge closer but was held captive by a now lifeless form that slumped, still chained, behind her. "Quickly! What are you waiting for?" The panic in her voice turned to despairing wrath. "HELP ME, YOU BITCH! YOU'LL BURN FOR THIS! YOU HEAR ME?! DAMN YOU!"

Her malevolent cries were drowned out by the infernal orchestra of fire. As the metal burnt the skin around the woman's middle, the third prisoner, now free, finally turned from the violence of the scene in front.

She ran. Crawled and scrambled, dodged and clambered over the dead and dying, her emaciated body helping her desperate rush for freedom. The skin on her arms and face burning red, beginning to crack and blister from the searing heat. Her eyes stung and wept, the caustic smoke clouding and stinging her vision and pouring into her lungs making her wheeze and splutter. Hands to her face, she fought to maintain consciousness. Then, a burst of fresh air. Blue through the red, grey and black. Hands outstretched, clawing and fighting through the fringes of the crowd, she collapsed into an empty space, onto her hands and knees, gasping, hacking, retching. Yet somehow still vigilant, still alert. Straight ahead, a passageway through the houses. Her lungs ached. Skin in rage. But she ran.

CHAPTER TWO

ON THE PEASANT'S WAY

Tolva's feet had been ripped open by the rough shingle of the track. Her now blood-stained fingers pulled fragments of stone from the shredded flaps of skin as she sat huddled on a clump of soft weeds at the way side. Grimacing, she picked another piece of grit from an oozing sore and poured a little cold water from her carrier over the wound to clean and soothe it. Her cloth bundle lay open beside her, untied from her shoulder. From the tumbled pile of eclectic possessions, she drew a roll of linen. This she wrapped carefully around her foot, partly as a bandage, partly as a marginally protective layer. The grass beside her, so painfully absent for the vast majority of her long journey, was damp from the morning dew. She had not slept last night and the damp chill had settled in her bones. Enough. Enough now. Tolva had set out to run away as far as she could from the city, from the past, from the horrors that vividly haunted her. The savage names and poisonous rumours. The bars and chains. The feel of fire and the smell of death. Enough. How long she had been walking she could not say. But she could go no further.

Behind her the road she had travelled stretched back, fading out of sight down a hillside before reappearing again in the distance through the heat haze, winding its way around a copse where she had last paused to momentarily take the weight from her ravaged feet. It had been some days since she had passed any kind of settlement, let alone anything that could pass as a town or village. Yet it had also been some days, or maybe weeks, since she could hear the beating of her own heart and taste bile whenever she sensed people nearby. On nights huddled between jutting roots, she could still hear the screams and feel the burning on her skin. She had run until she could run no more. Then she had walked, and walked, gathering some small possessions along the way, outrunning the horrors and memories. The peace and calm of the natural world around her was nourishing and rejuvenating. Harmonious whispers of song hung on the breeze, words of growth and new life. Streams and brooks trickled in furrows, spurred on by mossy stones that sent the playful water onwards, bringing mirth and laughter to the grasses that danced and swayed above. Breathing in, Tolva could hear tiny voices carried on the breeze, vulnerable but defiant: the deft song of the leaves dancing on the boughs of magisterial trees; the laughter of the grasses as they swayed in unison; the delighted gasps of the flowers as they turned their faces skyward, searching for the warmth and comfort of the sun; so many individual sounds that sang a song of harmony. She welcomed them, drew them in, a sensation deep in her stomach. She had no map to tell her where she was, or to guide her in where she was heading, but the Gods had allowed her to survive until now and so she trusted in them to renew her purpose.

A rustling noise to her left startled Tolva and she immediately tensed, knowing her own vulnerability. Movement further along the verge, on the other side of the way, but cumbersome and awkward, not stealthy or sinister. She squinted and her vision penetrated the shadow and foliage.

"I can hear your'n breathin', my dear," cackled a

voice riddled with time and dotage. Tolva stayed silent. "Oh, I've jumpsed you, my love! You stay put and Goldie will make amends, get you something for those sorely feet…"

Tolva was just beginning to wonder how this aged lady could possibly see her feet from the distance between them when the wrinkled, slouched shape shuffled from her tree-stump seat into the clear morning light. Tolva had time to study her as her walking stick scraped over the stone and cratered mud, the movement laboured, but her scratchy voice continued to holler out.

"Ha! I know you're wonderin' how I knew! Do not you worry deary, I'm no witch – I could tell it by the way you plonked your'nself down there on that grass."

It was then that Tolva noticed her eyes. They were yellowing with a grey pupil in each that had misted over; they looked in separate directions, bulging out from under directionless eyebrows that seemed to be swallowed by heavily wrinkled skin.

"Don't say much do you, pet? I know, you're probably a young'un who don't want to be bothered by a blathering crone like me! Ha!" She had now shuffled herself quite close to the seated runaway. "Or maybe you're one of them... One of them..." she faltered. The air had changed. Now the old lady felt vulnerable. "Are you...?" The words would not come. Falteringly, she backed away. "Sorry to have bothered you," she mumbled and with occasional looks back, she trundled on until she was lost to the rise and fall of the hill. Tolva watched her go. Strange lady. But at least she had distracted from the pain in Tolva's feet which had now somewhat abated for the time being. With memory of the unwanted acquaintance fresh in her mind, Tolva looked around her, knowing it was time to move on.

Further along the track, the route wandered its way under the cover of trees, leaving behind the rising sun over the fields. Ahead, she could see a lighter patch of woodland and perhaps a path that fell away to the right, falling lightly downhill away from the main way. Tolva carefully rebundled her few possessions and tied the cloth corners into a loop, swinging her crude pack over her shoulder. Pulling herself up on the gnarled bark of a tree, she took a few tentative stumbles forward, easing herself into the pain of walking. Step by step, she made her way onward, using the grass verge where possible, and edging towards the light ahead.

The tree cover broke over a crossroads of several paths. Tolva looked back along the course she had travelled, noticing that it was, by some distance, the widest and most trodden. A trade route, perhaps? Ahead, to her left, a squat standing stone blanketed with moss signalled the beginning of the way. The green adornment fell easily aside with a brush of her skeletal fingers: 'The Peasant's Way' it read. A wry smile passed over Tolva's lips at the aptness of the name, and then sighed with loss at the realisation that she had not smiled in… days? Weeks? Months? She stood again and raised her face to the warmth that floated through the canopy. A comforting, soothing warmth, not the searing heat of a blaze. She allowed the memory to linger. It did not scare or panic her. Not any more. It had given her strength.

As she opened her eyes, the silhouette of a signpost had crept its way across the sun. Shielding her eyes with her hand, she allowed the wooden structure to drift into focus. Ageing, allowing nature to coat it with hues of green and orange, only one arrow offered a destination and she focussed her attention on its finely carven lettering.

Fenwood.

The name was familiar. A distant conversation from a lifetime now past. A passing comment from a fleeting acquaintance. She knew it was a long way from where she had come. A place where people would not know her name. Where people would not make the same assumptions and judgements. Looking hastily around, there appeared to be no outlying villages or buildings and therefore, the settlement would be small. A warm feeling began stirring in her stomach. Excitement? Hope?

The sloped track was gravelled and well-trodden, crude but purposeful. It picked a cautious route through the blues, pinks and whites of wild flowers on either side, easing between two healthy rising hedgerows and falling gently away to the left in a curving slope. Tolva tried to walk on tiptoe to peer over the lush bushes as the sky emerged unbroken from the tree branches above. The height of the hedgerows teased her: short enough to hint at something beyond, but tall enough to keep its secrets hidden. Then a whisper of smoke drifted lazily on the breeze, enticing Tolva. Not the

smoke of a blaze. The smoke of hearth and home. Her
step quickened. And finally, as if in answer, the
hedgerow relented.

A settlement nestled itself into the valley, with
buildings topped with roofs of straw and wood, close
knit and neighbourly. Aside from the wisps of smoke
that coasted from several chimney-holes, the sense of
calm and tranquillity was so great that one could be
forgiven for thinking it lay dormant. Tolva stopped in
wonder. Gazing at the rooftops she could see that they
were enclosed, embraced even, by narrow woodland
that formed a protective circle around the buildings.
Outside of this, fertile fields stretched to the periphery
of her view and, now that she was really looking, figures
hard at work evolved from the mud and grass to stoop
and heave at the ground beneath their feet. They toiled
and paced in slow, methodical movements, not in
unison or rhythm, but nonetheless in harmony with the
other working figures and the land itself. Carefully,
respectfully. The fields, the ring of trees, the simple
wooden houses and buildings, all, somehow, seemed to
flow effortlessly into one another, as if part of the same
picture, the same design.

Only one building stood apart. Rising from the embracing boughs of luscious leaves, a stone castle dominated the skyline of the north eastern edge of the settlement. A white tower rose high above, the ramparts of the base also visible over the trees, with a forest (rather than fields) stretching out beyond. Despite its obvious material difference, it did not seem at odds with its surroundings; perhaps the greenish hue of age made it akin to the natural world around. A jewel in an untainted crown. It had an unmistakable majesty, an ethereal, ageless quality that stirred a reverence and longing deep within Tolva's soul. She felt now that some force had drawn her from the Peasant's Way to this place. Fixing her gaze, she whispered something inaudible to the wind before readjusting her shouldered bundle and picked her steps along the shingle track, this time with purpose.

CHAPTER THREE

FENWOOD

The path meandered its way, like a lazy river, through a thoroughfare of suffocating branchlets and welcoming briars. Tolva glanced continuously to her left, hoping to catch a glimpse of the smooth wood and woven straw of the buildings; of Fenwood. Yet the path had entered a fairytale grotto, nature's tunnel, and the enclosed path drifted through the undergrowth. Her feet no longer bothered her, and she even began to skip along the track. With her attention drawn to the unseen down in the valley, overhanging branches scratched her arms and head, but she paid them no heed and followed the path, keenly looking for a gap in the branches to peer through.

Turning a corner, the track finally emerged from its thicket. Tolva almost gasped as she stopped. Rising above the treetops, she glimpsed in the distance an ivory tower glinting in the spring morning sun, like a beacon. And just as suddenly as it had appeared, it was gone again, the teasing sight masked by a breeze-blown bough. The roofs that she had seen from the top of the valley had disappeared below the treeline, but homely smoke was still evident, drifting like a seasonal whisper that now carried with it the occasional sounds of market cries and farmers' commands. The feeling that swelled in Tolva's stomach was something akin to happiness, but greater: awe.

The descending path had cleared its way from the undergrowth and began to pick a route along hedgerows adjoining fields that housed livestock and crops. Storehouses and sheds had begun to appear in these outlying areas, good solid buildings of wood with straw roofs. Yet, unlike the structures she was used to seeing and living or working in, the walls were not of stone but of mud composite, smoothed and washed with white, as if nature were gifting the people safety.

"Your presence here is so strong," she whispered.

The wholesome breeze breathed life back into her legs and soul, and when a bearded man with a weather-beaten face and simple clothes waved from behind a small herd of cattle, Tolva found herself smiling and waving enthusiastically in reply. Somewhat embarrassed, she caught herself and, when the farmer began to approach her, she dropped her head and quickened her pace, pretending that she had not seen his intent.

The firmed path continued to something more purposeful, being joined by further tracks; more and more people passed by. Tolva was forced to nod and smile with a warmth that was at first a front, but soon melted to genuine welcome, such was the greetings she received from the open, beaming faces. She noted their clothing; in the city where she had been, garments were cut and lined and woven using silks and expensive fabrics, the extravagance a symbol of status. But not here. Simple cloth, simple design. Practical and comfortable. And she could not help but admire them.

Several paths converged into an open grass area, well maintained, akin to an entrance hall. But no one's attention stayed there for long. Standing tall and triumphant in the foreground were great pillars of oak soaring to the sky in a burst of luscious, curved foliage. There were many, stretching as far as the eye could see in each direction and in between hedgerows, making the barrier impenetrable. Tolva had never seen anything like it.

At the centre of the clearing, flanked by guardians of oak, a pair of large, carved doors stood invitingly open. Ornate depictions of birds and branches and produce adorned the panels, representing the land that lay beyond; an embodiment of the simplicity and beauty of life and the symbiosis of Nature and Man. Running her fingers caressingly over the wood as she passed anonymously through the entranceway, Tolva soaked up every detail. Stepping through onto the mud paths and pebbled streets, her dark hair flicked this way and that as she took in every sensation: the smells of baking and fresh flowers; the roar of furnaces and children in the throes of gameplay; honest faces of warmth and toil. Had she been searching for somewhere particular, Fenwood would have seemed a labyrinth of winding streets and wholesome troves. Her wandering was aimless, soaking up the atmosphere, drinking in the air. The hustle and bustle was a far cry from the solitary days on the road, and the weeks and months in the far away city, but here she sensed safety and comfort. People who passed by smiled and nodded with warmth and humanity, not derision and fear.

Finding dry hay bales in an open shed, Tolva spent her first night in Fenwood open to the elements but tucked away from prying eyes. Unlike many of the nights along the aimless routes she had travelled, that night she slept easily, peacefully. When the cockerels hailed the morn, she lay with eyes closed and listened to the sounds of the world until the clacking of tools and chatter of voices grew closer. Quietly, she snuck away to the cover of the nearby trees and watched the men preparing their work for the day. On the way back to the uneven, gravelled streets, she refreshed herself with water from a street-corner fountain, but the rumbling of her stomach could not be quelled by the cool water alone. Her pack had emptied of food and people of the town were not in the habit of throwing out scraps to the street for worry of rats and disease. There was no market to ask for samples and she was too proud to beg. Midday arrived with the smell of bread and cooking fat wafting around the muddle of streets. Tolva had known hunger along the road, but not only had she managed her scant provision well, she had thought nothing of stealing from men who had attempted to take advantage of her. But not here. She could not.

The streets became busier as people completed their jobs for the day and Tolva's weakening body was swept up in the growing tide of people making their way to where the source of the aromas seemed to be. First there was the bakery on the corner, shelves lined with soft, warm bread and cakes drizzled with melted, colourful sugars. Then, the butchers, who cooked up mutton and suckling pig and rolls with minced pig-meat. Finally, a large building, set with flowers in boxes and a large painted door in the centre, opening and closing with a frequent flow of visitors. It was a large inn that dominated a courtyard in the western dwellings of the inner reaches of the town.

Tolva gingerly pushed open the hefty wooden door of The Oaks. Immediately she was hit with warmth and a barrage of raucous laughter that reached around the door. Hesitating, she peered round into the bustling room. In the centre, a carved bar thrust out into the floorspace that was covered in an array of circular and rectangular tables, each of which was surrounded by a variety of mix-match chairs. Despite her trepidation, Tolva slid in unnoticed and picked a route between legs and backs and swigging arms.

"I've not seen your face around here before," delved Roker, the publican, as he slid a cup of apple-water across the bar to the avianesque lady. "I definitely would have remembered..." he continued with a nervous smile, but stopped as she looked up and her eyes met his. Her face softened and the landlord lingered near her as he ran a cloth around the rims of the collected cups and glasses. The main open room of the inn was bustling with jovial faces of labouring folk enjoying well-earned refreshment at the close of another toiling day. Tables packed the area, seat backs touching as tables filled up with groups of colleagues and friends; serving boys and girls often forced to walk the long way round to serve frothing glasses of beer or collect drained glasses to return to the bar. The Oaks, the central inn, was popular; a meeting place for the people of Fenwood, much aided by the welcoming attitude of Roker and his young son who warmly accepted all locals and travellers to their drinking house where tales of adventures and heroes were as familiar as important chatter about village life and the weather. Indeed, the walls were adorned with paintings and sketches of well-known Fenwood figures, past and present, alongside impressions of familiar and memorable ceremonies. And now, Tolva perched on a tall stool at the bar itself, informally reserved for those patrons who were eating and drinking alone; the community feel of the inn meant that these seats were usually vacant.

"I have travelled a long way," she said, brushing strands of dark hair from her face, a comment not intended as a conversation starter, merely to fill the silence.

"Where from?" Roker politely enquired. Her vacant gaze told him that no answer would be given. "Why here?" he ventured further.

"Here… Fenwood…" Tolva turned and looked around the tavern. People talking, laughing, playing card games. Community. Harmony.

"It's fine" – his voice interjected her thoughts – "you don't have to tell me."

"No." She turned back to him, not able to stop herself from relaxing again at his kindly face. "No, it's just that… I hadn't planned to come here." The answer did not satisfy. "Something… drew me here."

"No family or relatives?" he offered. By now, the barman was redrying the same cups. She shook her head. "Where are you staying?"

"I had not… thought that far ahead." She steeled herself against the suggestion that she was sure would come; it never did. Instead, the man's kindly eyes narrowed, pondered her face for a moment, before lowering his voice.

"I know a goodly family who may be able to help you out." He set down the cup. "Have your drink, eat some food, and then I'll send my boy, Hopps, to show you the way."

"Thank you. So much." For a moment she was overwhelmed. "This place, Fenwood… Everyone is so happy, and seemingly care free."

"We are lucky," replied Roker, the contentment shining in the lines of his face. "The Gods have granted us a land that provides, and in turn we nurture it. We have much to be thankful for."

Tolva looked at the man, unsure whether to feel sympathy or adoration for the man's naivety.

"Thank you, too, for your kindness. I'm afraid, I… erm…" she began, but Roker knew how the sentence ended. There was something mysterious about the newcomer, certainly, but there was also a sincerity and vulnerability that drew Roker in. With a smirk he playfully tossed the grubbied cloth toward her.

"You could start by bringing me those cups and bowls from the table in the far corner, by the window… Maybe give it a once over with the rag?"

She blinked several times, her green eyes making sense of the situation. Roker wondered if he had made a mistake and reached a rough hand back across the bar for the cloth. Tolva's short, talon-like nails rapped the wood as she snatched the browning rag into her hand. She returned the smile.

"Will do." A genuine laugh. "Boss."

*   *   *

Her arrival caused very little stir. Tolva blended in with the world around her and Fenwood life. She was polite and attentive around the tavern, chatting to the regular customers, as if she had always been there. Yet, in the weeks that followed, she formed no close friendships, revealed nothing of her past, laughed away any attempts to delve beneath the surface. Often she ate with Roker and Hopps at the end of the day, once the customers had left, grateful for the food and for the company. After they had hugged her and thanked her for her work, she took the coin offered as payment and made her way through the quiet streets, relishing the peace to clear her mind after the closeness of noise at the inn. The kindly Goodward family had granted her a key to her rooms, impressed as they were that she was quiet and tidy, paid rent on time, and never brought home strangers.

The tavern allowed Tolva to settle quietly, away from much public scrutiny but still able to become known. She had worked in bars and inns before, in larger, louder cities, where wandering hands and drunken tongues had come as part of the job. Fights had been commonplace. Every working day had been a risk to the lives of those young women who worked there. Tolva carried those experiences for the first few days as she moved uneasily between the abundant tables, dodging chairs and flailing arms of animated, jubilant patrons. Her green eyes were wary, darting around furtively, looking for dangers which never materialised from the shadows that only she saw. The cloth remained a fixture in her hand, a prop that she clung to. Slowly, over the coming months, she allowed her smile, and her voice, to show.

"Fooooooood!" A deep, gravelly female bellow uttered from the smoky recess behind the bar, a faceless voice. Tolva's ears pricked up; the people of the room remained oblivious. She cast her eyes toward the far wall and saw the steaming bowl sat on the food shelf. Smiling at the men and women nearby, she reached over their shoulders and collected up the ale jars before working her way back through the legged obstacles where she deposited them at the bar. Being careful not to burn her fingers, she lifted the hot tureen of broth onto her tray and turned quickly, too quickly. Her body collided with the stout, solid frame of a man with a long, oiled beard and light tanned coat, sending her crashing to the stone floor. Ignoring the pain in her knees, Tolva instinctively braced herself for the downward force of a fist or the dull blow of a boot. The calm hand on her shoulder made her jump and lash out.

"My dear, are you hurt?" The tone was sympathetic, genuine. Looking up, the first thing she saw was a greasy slab of pork fat sticking to the man's jacket pocket and drips of meaty broth cascading from his coiffured facial hair, but his eyes and manner carried none of the threat she had expected. Her relief brought guilt.

"Oh sir, I am so sorry! I did not… I had no idea… I…"

"Young lady, I am unharmed – you, on the other hand, have taken a tumble. Your knees are grazed. Come, sit with us a moment…" He took her gently by the arm, ready to lead Tolva to a nearby table.

"No, no, I must get back…"

"Nonsense. Sit with us. Roker, Hopps, your darling… What is your name, dear?"

She almost gave him a name that was not her own.

"Ha… Tolva."

"…Darling Tolva has fallen. Could you please bring some cloth… Clean cloth, please…"

As the stranger carefully daubed her grazed knee, stinking as he was of fatty stew in a coat now ruined with cooking oils, Tolva realised how far she was from the cities of her former life.

As she allowed Fenwood to soften her heart, the more Tolva began to embrace the daily routines and traditions that surrounded her. On sun-basked mornings she would take the sales tray from under the counter and, hanging it around her neck, stock the front with fresh apple wine and go into the street outside to offer samples and greet locals. Roker knew that he could trust her with people, that she held a power which drew both men and women to her, and began to send his new green-eyed starlet on more public and challenging assignments;: running the stall on market day; feeding crowds at outdoor ceremonies and helping children create their lunches at family events. But secretly, she longed to see the shining towers, grand halls and endless corridors of the castle.

Standing under the eaves of the forest, Tolva subconsciously ran her fingertips over the rough, gnarled bark, grounding herself as she looked out over the cultivated fields and thatched rooftops. Despite having lived in the town for the change of three seasons, she could not yet call Fenwood her home; that was an ideal she had never been able to use for any of the places she had lived. At least she was, or felt, safe. The danger she sensed in the air was not a malice toward her, more a pervading sense of the chaos of nature, the balance that must come with the peace of the land. Looking up higher still, the towers of the castle dimmed in the setting sun, no longer white but a pink-orange hue that reflected the falling of the day. Whilst her mind and body needed the nourishment of nature, part of her longed to experience the grandeur and power that channelled through the grand, stately castle, sitting imperious on a hillside overlooking the deferential town below. Leaning back against the tree, she closed her eyes and allowed herself to visualise the interiors: soft, silken linen against rough stone; the history of the realm painstakingly embroidered in hanging tapestries on the walls of magisterial banqueting halls; subservient, silent ghosts treading lightly in the shadows of the corridors.

A burning sensation ripped through her eyes, causing Tolva to squint; *blink*, and the vision changed. The howling of a wolf that became the roaring of a fire, and a castle descending into flame. *Blink*, she was soaring above woodland, riding on the wind. Clean air and freedom. Searching for… no, knowing something was below, running through the undergrowth; a kindred spirit, a twin soul.

With a sharp intake of breath she came back to her

senses. Tolva turned her head from the dwellings and into the forest, eyes piercing the gathering gloom. Often, on her way from the inn to her residence after a day of cleaning and collecting, her feet would bring her to the forest and venture inside. She was not afraid of the forest as others were, even as the dusk was setting in and the shadows lengthened to night. The leaves and branches whispered a different song. Tonight, as her hands gently eased the encroaching branches from her path, she listened to the sultry welcome.

"I'm coming," she chuckled, and allowed the brushwood curtain to close behind her.

*   *   *

"Welcome, all, to the Grain Blessing." The Master of Agriculture spread his arms in an act of communal embrace to the crowd that had gathered in the lane outside the entrance to Fenwood Mill. Sweat ran down his bald head that had much to do with nerves rather than heat, with the beads being lost in the curls of his bushy grey beard. His beige waistcoat contrasted in its muted tone to the bright purple jacket of the Master of Ceremonies who stood at his side. The blessing of grain was a significant act in the Fenwood calendar; there was a reliance on a good harvest, and anything that could be done to appease the Gods was enthusiastically undertaken. The waiting onlookers were buoyant but reverent, acknowledging the importance of the event. Whilst it was a ceremony and not a celebration, there was still a need for refreshment and many carried a cup of apple wine and suckling pig in a bread roll.

Further down Mill Lane, on a wooded footway nestled between two horse paddocks, running alongside the river, Tolva and Hopps stood behind a low wooden table, passing out food and drink to those who made their way to the mill. Hopps' youthful exuberance was infectious, bouncing from one foot to the other, his smile and chatter magnetic. Often he wandered his way into the centre of the track itself, greeting folk regularly by name and drawing them in to purchase the Oaks' wares. Behind him at the table, occasionally glancing up and smiling from behind her long, black hair, Tolva poured from pewter jugs filled with cloudy juice and tonged succulent meat into fresh rolls. It was not her first event but she had not yet the outward confidence to put herself into the public traffic. In this way she and

Hopps made a good team, and she enjoyed being out in the town. Or village? City? The people of Fenwood used all three terms, seemingly interchangeable, and she could not yet fathom the size of the lands, inhabited and farmed, to make her own judgement.

"Thank you, Tolva." A kindly old man nodded, a fine drooping pipe between his lips. She baulked at the use of her name but recovered quickly to return the pleasantry.

"You are very welcome, sir."

"Fernly. Fernly Datchett." His grin was joyous, genuine.

"You're welcome, Mr Datchett." Tolva smiled.

A ripple of excitement could be heard from the end of the lane and murmurs of something extraordinary reached the latecomers who had been unable to resist the wafting aromas of cooked pig fat. People quickened their step and hurried on to the mill, not knowing why but keen to be part of the apparent increase in magnitude. Hopps craned his neck from the far side of the stony track but the curve of the path rendered a visual impossible. Looking back at Tolva, he pleaded silently with wide eyes.

"Of course, you can go," she giggled, warmly.

"You're the best!" he yelled over his shoulder as he disappeared between bodies, overtaking them with an impish delight. Tolva continued to turn the pig meat over in the cooking juices, keeping the meat moist, chuckling inwardly to herself. But she was startled to hear her name being called from the curve ahead.

"Tol! Tolva!"

Hopps stood on one leg, a look of sheer delight shining in his young eyes.

"She's here! She's come." He paused to catch his breath. "The Queen!"

She moved with such poise and grace. The way she floated through the crowd; her greying hair, like silver, cascading in natural, tumbling curls down her back. Effortlessly turning her head this way and that to greet each besotted bystander, not flinching as people occasionally reached out to touch her. Regal and queenly, yet still somehow of this place, of her people. Tolva watched on from the very edges of the group, mesmerised. For a moment, the white-robed monarch was lost from sight amongst the many bobbing heads and waving arms of the growing mass, only to reappear

again on the steps up to the dais. The Master of
Ceremonies bowed his head courteously as she passed,
but the bald-headed compere at his side began to get to
one knee in over-dramatic reverence. The Queen
laughed warmly and took his arm.

"Oh the Gods, you are all too kind!" she said,
turning from the Master of Agriculture to the adoring
onlookers. A hush descended quickly, so keen were they
to hear her speak. "My good sir has already welcomed
you here for this important event in our calendar, and I
do not wish to interrupt the ceremony. The King and I"
– his absence had already been noted by many –
"wanted to mark this moment of blessing, that we may
celebrate with you the abundance of the year ahead."
Her words were met with rapturous applause. With
good grace, she stepped back, allowing the minister to
take up his long-rehearsed monologue on the history of
grain-growing in Fenwood.

Tolva could not take her eyes off the magnificent
woman who now appeared to show great interest in the
ramblings of the man who stood at the centre of the
dais. Many of the celebratory onlookers watched on,
their eyes drawn from the monarch to the speaker to

the surroundings, and yet only Tolva witnessed the flicker in the eyes of the Queen as she felt a disturbance, an unease; casting a quick nervous eye over the crowd, she noticed nothing untoward and brushed rolling hair from her eyes before returning with noble interest to the event at hand. Tolva moved her head from behind the tall man in front of her. Her breathing was inexplicably short. Her heartrate quickened. Tolva turned, wanting to escape the intensity that tightened around her chest, and headed through the crowd back in the direction of the table still littered with bottles and plates.

Looking out from the dais, the Queen saw only the last steps of a woman in a skirt that caught the wind as she disappeared from sight round the corner of the tree-lined road.

CHAPTER FOUR
THE HOF

Seasons changed. The transformation of colours and fall of leaves heralded celebrations of life and the passage of time in Fenwood's traditions and ceremonies. Rituals began to embrace the darkness and chaos that came with the gathering gloom and symbolism of death and the macabre. Children dressed up in comical, ghostly portrayals, making light of the fears and spiritual turbulence of the time. The sun slowly dropped each day, hiding behind the silhouetted treetops as the moon fought for control of the skies.

A cold and manipulative wind pierced the misted glow of the nervous morning sunlight. It picked at the vulnerable wild flowers that dared to poke their anxious heads out above the frost that formed on the ground, a restrictive blanket that caged the earth. The tendrils of mist crept their way down the labyrinthian streets, searching out the corners where it skulked in quiet menace. It lingered in doorways and gathered in dead ends. Very few people were about in the hazy morning light. The mist threatened to overrun, to conquer, until it rounded a corner to the central square and instantly dissolved against the onslaught of noise and activity. Industrious bodies weaved around each other in a diligent dance, carrying boxes and shifting packages to tables and standing boxes that had been positioned to direct human traffic around the stalls. It was early and the merchants were still setting up, but already there were spices and ornaments and colourful silks. It was market day.

Tolva stood on the corner of the square outside Mallory's cigar shop, the sign in the shape of a smoking pipe swaying and creaking above her head. She had arrived early, allowed the mist to trickle around her ankles as the stallholders and travellers had begun arriving, and kept an eye on the goods on offer should anything catch her eye. She would be selling a new, experimental gooseberry wine; no stall, but the sales shelf leant against the wall beside her with bottles of the new brew ready to be loaded and decanted. It had been rumoured that the Queen would be making an appearance at the market today and Tolva had volunteered to carry the heavy shoulder-strapped shelf for the day, but knew it would be worth it if the regal figure herself arrived. Yet, as the central Fenwood square began to fill with patrons and proprietors, Tolva could see no sign of a queenly dignitary or royal-crested garments. Her head bowed in disappointment.

She sensed the man before she saw him. A consciousness, an aura. Even amongst the mass of bodies, stuttering and bending around market stalls, she knew him. There was something in the way he moved around the market square that drew her attention to him. An awkwardness in his hulking frame and a quietness in his immensity. The way in which his oversized hands held items and goods with such tenderness. How his jaw rolled, chewing on some unseen root, in such an animalistic fashion. Before she realised, she had placed the carrying shelf down against a wall and was following at a distance, but something drew her to him; a power that she could not fathom or place. Despite her striking appearance, she was able to blend into the shadows and merge into the crowds. Passing as he did with ease through the jostling and bumbling hordes, people noted him but looked or stepped away. And, in turn, he seemed to hold no camaraderie with the townsfolk, existing in the same place but feeling no need to engage with them. She inhaled, eyelids flickering shut. No malice, no ill will, but no need to conform. Of them, but not with them. She opened her eyes again. Breathed out.

With his pack of fresh produce slung over his sturdy shoulder, the broad figure made his way between the tobacconists and the tanners, navigating the paths through the Fenwood streets without thought until the trodden street stones gave way to muddied tracks. Tolva paused at the fence post, half concealed by the emerging hedgerow. She watched as his powerful physique blended into the surrounding bushes and fields. Still she could not pinpoint the sensation she felt. Perhaps she sensed that he was clearly an outsider, like her? Looking around, the pervading sense of tranquillity was almost palpable, aided by the soundscape of birdsong and content field workers. The land was unbroken by houses… and a thought interrupted her reflections… then, where was he going?

Overhead, a solitary raven swooped low and circled,

almost as if wanting to be noticed. Tolva's eyes lifted to the skies, connecting with the black bird. Spreading its wings, it let the wind carry its fragile body forward before drifting in the direction of the forest. Tolva now focussed her eyes on the woodland opening some distance in front of her and set off, with purpose but not pace.

The hanging boughs and canopy branches blocked out the sun's influence and darkening the brushwood around her. To her left and right the undergrowth grew denser, walls and barriers of brown and green rising to restrict her movement. Paths ran in different directions, beauty in chaos, wild and unpredictable. Yet, despite the thicketed disarray, despite not having the broad man in her sights, her inner eye sensed the direction he was heading, soaring above, watchful. Making her way through the thickening woodland, she moved branches from her path, confidently following her intuition, her compass. Every now and again she glanced skyward as the bird glided across the forest-roof skylights. She was closing in now. What she would say to him she did not know, but his earthen pull was powerful, a riveting fateful attraction.

Somewhere amongst the clouds, the black bird cawed. A disruption. Tolva hesitated at a split path, her foot sliding on soft mud. Looking to the left she could begin to see the corner of a wooden, lumber-built structure befitting the aura of the man she had followed. But now a sensation drew her to the other way. Gazing through the restrictive green hands above, the bird was nowhere to be seen through the broken leaf canopy. Turning, craning her neck, her green eyes clung to the unknown path, searching for an answer. Inhaling through her nose, she closed her eyes. Grey. Blurred. Shadows. But a voice rode on the swaying of the branches.

I am here. I will protect you.

With one last glance at the carven, wooden homestead, she followed her instincts.

The track soon became nothing more than a disruption in the wild land. Tolva picked her way through the groping arms of forgotten trees, spurred on by the beating of her heart. The voice in the shadows became two, three, more, some in tongues she could not understand, some speaking words of hope and kindness, some rising up in warning. Swirling echoes of lives lived and pain endured. They rose and fell with the *doom doom doom* in her chest. Still she pushed on, attempting to shut out the building cacophony of noise, singling out the force that compelled her. And suddenly, as if someone had snuffed out a candle, all noise ceased. Calm. Clarity.

It was not a clearing nor an open area where the scrub had stood back in grand ceremony. The beaten way Tolva had been following blundered on as a trodden channel through wild grasses, leading to a crude door constructed of intertwined sticks and reed-like grass blades. Surrounding the entrance, the structure was careful but unskilled; larger fallen boughs erected vertically and bound with hand-spun twine and muddied clay. It had been built from the world around it by loving hands. As Tolva stood in wide-eyed delight, she sensed the energy of the forest here and, arms outstretched, allowed it to flow through her. Her mother had told her about places like this many years ago; a spiritual centre where people could gather together and pray to the Gods or immerse themselves in Nature's power. A hof.

Stepping forward, Tolva felt almost breathless.

Subduing the reticence that rose from her stomach, she moved through the grasses to an outline in the threaded branches, gently trying to gain entrance. The door gave her some resistance, as if being pushed from within. With renewed effort it relinquished its battle and gave way, granting her access. Suddenly, she could sense the danger inside with the creaking of the woven hinges.

The wolf was already standing, baring sharp teeth, a low growl in its throat. Tolva could see penetrating yellow eyes in the gloom before her own adjusted enough to make out the alert body position, ready to strike, to kill. Panic gripped her and she shifted her eyes from side to side, unable to get her feet to move backward through the doorway she had come. The she-wolf sensed fear, desperation, and bent lower with a gnashing of savagery. In her furtive glances about the room, Tolva suddenly saw three cub faces peering from a long-dormant hearth on the far wall. Now, as she looked back at the wolf mother, her eyes read very differently. Closing them, she channelled her mind on the wolf. Her words were clear and authoritative.

"I will not harm you."

The wolf recoiled. Tolva raised her hand in an open-palmed display of peace.

"Do not be afraid."

Raising her shoulders from the ground the wolf straightened her back, still wary but no longer on the offence. A gruff snort offered her response.

Who are you?

Chancing the initiative, Tolva lowered her hand. Their eyes searched each other for answers, for understanding, for truths. Tolva's eyelids fluttered shut and she drew in a purposeful breath. When she opened them again there was a slight change in the colours of her vision; her words were no longer spoken aloud but the wolf heard them clearly.

"I am called Tolva. I mean you and your cubs no harm."

Her yellow eyes growing pale, the wolf turned her head back to the vulnerable babes huddled together in the fireplace. They mewed and pawed at each other, jostling, vying for position. Looking back at the human, framed in the light of the doorway, she sniffed the air for the scent of danger. Nothing. She let her jaw hang and panted, but never altered her gaze.

Do you have… pups?

Tolva gently shook her head.

"No. But I will. One day."

Tentatively padding forward, the wolf sniffed again, this time of the human.

Yes. The Mother is strong in you.

A moment of real understanding and respect passed between them. Outside, the forest leaned in, eavesdropping. The wolf glanced back at her cubs, who clambered over each other, squabbling and shuffling for comfort. Both Tolva and the wolf mother looked on before the animal turned back to the human, keen to know why she had come to this place.

The air changed.

Her dark grey fur bristled and she moved back onto her haunches.

Go. Danger.

Tolva had sensed it too. Grabbing at a knotted branch in the door, she yanked the door open again in a motion to flee. Standing in her way were a man and woman dressed heavily in animal hide. Upon their faces lay the marks of violent battle, war paint and greed. A startled moment passed between the three humans, of intrigue to realisation.

It was the savage woman who moved first, flinching,

raising her curved blade swiftly up above her head and swinging it down toward the defenceless figure in the doorway. Tolva reacted quickly, instinctively, slamming the door. The force of the blow deflected off the weathered boughs, glancing to the side. As the door reached the frame, the warrior-woman's hand became trapped between. With a yelp of stinging pain and surprise, the blade dropped to the floor. In a moment, Tolva had thrown her body against the debris-mottled door. The sound of agonising frustration from outside grew as the hunter struggled to be free. A spearhead crashed through the twigs, grazing Tolva's ribs. Her breath came in sharp rasps and she searched the room for answers, solutions. The wolf's head movements were similarly frantic. Scampering forward, her paws pushed the shining metal blade in the direction of the human, straining against the force on the other side of the door. Again the spear penetrated the foliage, accompanied by the frenzied screams of a female voice who fought to free her trapped hand. In the melee, Tolva felt the weight on the door lessen and quickly leant forward to snatch up the weapon. Finding the handle warm, she looked at the metal, notched and marked through use, and steeled herself with the will to use it. Closing her eyes, she visualised the figures on the other side of the door. When she opened them, the wolf had lowered her head, eyes blazing, sensing opportunity.

Attack.

Her fangs bared. Menacing growl in her throat.

They came to kill.

Tolva breathed with her.

Attack.

The first blow from the blade sunk deep into the trapped wrist, severing flesh, veins, tendons and erupting maroon blood. The hand shook with shock but could no longer fight to free itself. The second blow struck the bone. A yellow hue burned in the maiden's eyes and the wolf roared in sensed victory. The third blow brought the hand thudding to the floor, rolling in the powdery mud. The scream from outside rose above the growl of the wolf who barked in warning of further attack. Frantic footsteps in trampled undergrowth disappeared in whimpers into the distance. Tolva tried to quell her lust for vengeance, still backed into the door. The wolf glanced over her shoulder at the bundle of fur still huddled for protection in the recess on the far wall. She padded the dusty ground, picking up the dismembered hand between her teeth and carried it toward her cubs. Wavering, she paused and looked back at the panting, wide-eyed woman, blade in hand, still dripping to the floor.

Go. Do not come here.

Outside, there was no sign of the savages other than the dark puddle at the entrance to the hof, and the soiled knife that Tolva had dropped in her desperation for clean air. The light momentarily stung her eyes but the breeze soothed her still bristling skin. Behind her, the wolf mother had slunk back into the shadows as the door closed on the chaos. Overhead, the raven could be seen circling, gliding serenely on the wind along the Downs.

"Oh dear'n me, my love, a fine mess that is." A scratchy, wizened voice from beyond the long, wild grasses. Tolva stepped carefully forward. There, perched on a cut log, an old crone sat twisting and knotting twine. Narrowing her eyes, she felt certain she had seen the lady before, but the face seemed to change with each angle and movement.

"You saw what happened?" Tolva asked, not

knowing what she wished to gain from the exchange. But the gnarled woman smiled to herself and focussed again on her craft. Suddenly voice came from her, stronger and clearer than before.

"Blood has been spilt in the hof, and the old Gods will be angered. Beware, Tolva of the Fire, for 'ere you are wolf mother blood must be spilt again." The crone looked up from under wrinkled brows. Tolva's face, stuck with sweat and matted fringe, looked concerned, confused.

"What do you mean?" the younger lady asked, searching in the uncertainty for reality.

"You can feel it," returned the old figure, balanced naturally on the stump, "you sense all things." Her misty eyes glanced skyward. "Where are your'n eyes, pretty thing?" Tolva raised her own gaze through the tree canopy, but when she brought her focus back, the old woman's clouded pupils were fixed on her.

"I feel it," she whispered in a cracked voice toward the woman, thinly knotted rope still running through her wrinkled fingers.

"...but others are afraid of that power," finished the voice from the tree stump.

Tolva nodded, and looked again back in the direction of the crude, wooden structure. A moment of understanding passed between the two figures. For a moment, a brilliance swept over the old woman's eyes and she saw clearly. Reaching out, their hands touched.

"Go carefully." Pause. "Tolva. One who has been touched by fire."

Tolva watched in silence as the crone settled her crafts into a hessian bag which was slung across her back. Knotted fingers gripped the tree stump as she steadied herself into a stooped standing position and began shuffling her way along the path through the forest. For a final time, Tolva looked back at the hof, pondering the prophetic words that had been spoken. Turning her gaze back to the trodden path, she retraced her steps to Fenwood, She did not pass the wizened old lady along the way.

*   *   *

Something had changed. The balance had shifted. For some time there had been peace and harmony, but now Tolva sensed a growing chaos. Standing in an open woodland glade, past the reaches of Fenwood, the voice of the trees was disquieting and almost nervous. The incident at the hof had not deterred her from walks in the forest, but now she listened attentively, warily. She had known disorder, violence, and fallen victim to it; now she was determined to embrace it, harness it, in some small sense to control it.

CHAPTER FIVE
OF TRADITIONS AND TOWERS

From her position towards the end of the procession of carts, horses and goods-laden stooped bodies, Tolva's view of the road to the castle was restricted to the stoned path and manicured hedgerows that led from Fenwood town. The great white towers stood to the north-west of the fields and dwellings, set aside so as to command respect as a position of power, but close enough to still feel a connection with the people and the land.

"Miss Tolva," called Hopps' bubbly young voice from the back of his father's abundant cart, "can you see it yet?"

She smiled at him.

"No, sweet boy. Not yet." He craned his head round to try and peer over the boxes of elderflower cordial and pear wine that were piled on to the horse cart. She laid her hand on his knee, partly to show her affection and partly to suggest he should not move around so much for fear of falling to the ground. He sighed, but with a grin born of curiosity and excitement.

The line of driven produce began to make its way up an incline, the bushes and trees on each side now falling away as the track started to climb the hill that formed the base of the castle, aiding its prominence and elevated position. The early morning wisps of cloud were beginning to stretch to nothingness. With the sun now warming their backs and shadows stretching in front, the bathing light fell on the white bricks that rose magnificently from the apex of the hill. Tolva hid the change in her breathing and glanced up to the boy; Hopps understood instantly and scrambled from the cart into her arms so that he could take in the sight. Time slowed. They clung to each other, united in awe.

It was more than just a castle. It was an icon. A symbol. A home. A fortress. History. Tradition. Reverence. In the sun's rays, its enlightened glow gave the white towers and walls an ethereal and other-worldly appearance. The entranceway sat within the centre of a large wall, a solid foundation of white stone with an archway holding creaking wooden doors. Upon its battlements stood another solid layer, smaller and central to the base; this pattern was repeated, like neatly stacked blocks, each atop the next, and so it reached to the sky. As they walked slowly closer, the traders craned their necks further, mouths aghast, breath stolen, eyes sparkling.

By the time those at the front of the cavalcade had reached the walls, the great oak doors had creaked open on their hand-crafted wooden hinges and the visiting parade had been welcomed through the archway and into a central courtyard. As Tolva passed under she took in each detail of the stonework, letting her fingertips glide over the smooth coldness of the wall. Up close, the glorious white that had shone from a distance was cracked, dirtied, tarnished. She touched the imperfections and then, checking no one was looking, placed her fingers to her tongue. Secrets. The castle had a voice.

"I'm listening," she whispered.

"What was that?" called Hopps.

Startled at being caught out, she flashed an insincere smile, and pointed ahead into the courtyard. The boy looked up and gasped.

The courtyard was not large, but welcoming; still white, but bedecked with vibrant climbing plants and flowers, taking the attention away from the practicalities of doorways, storage rooms and resources, necessaries that were hidden in plain view. With the arrival of so many guests, servants were busily ushering and carrying and being overly polite. Hopps' head darted this way and that, looking at everything he could.

"Tol! Tol!" he cried out excitedly. "Look… Look…!"

But she was not looking. She remained still. Far overhead a raven glided into view, circling the concourse, swooping down over the roofs of outbuildings, skimming the towers, finally perching on a window sill. Inside, a lady dressed in an expensive green silk dress gazed into a full-length looking glass, pulling the material tight over her stomach. Suddenly she had the unnerving sensation of being watched and turned sharply to the window. The raven cawed, turning its head on an angle, observing her. Somehow the lady felt exposed under its gaze. Then it flapped its wings and was lost to the hubbub of the melee below.

"What are you looking at?" Hopps' voice snapped

Tolva out of her trance. She glanced up, taken aback. "What do you see?"

She looked away, absently. "Everything."

*   *   *

Closed away, high above the courtyard, the lady fingered the fine diadem and tried to focus her attention back on the positive energy that she was trying to build in the mirror, but her attention had been broken by the invasion of the carrion bird. From the courtyard below the sound of her visitors clambered up the tower walls. Intrigue took over. Picking the train of her dress from the floor, she crossed the polished stone to the window frame, careful not to place her hand where the raven had been, and peered down to the hustle and bustle below. Holding her long, shining hair off her face, she allowed her ponderous gaze to drift this way and that over the eclectic group that had arrived, invited, from the town. A pinch of joy struck her cheek. She genuinely relished days like these, when the common folk were allowed inside the castle walls. There was always so much joy and awe and wonder, reminding her that she should never take this place, these people, for granted, as she once had. But not now. Good people. Decent people. Her people. And she their Queen.

Soaring inquisitively above, she saw the black bird again, silhouetted against the wisping clouds in the bright morning sky. Long ago she would have felt jealous of its freedom, of being able to roam far and wide, feeling the wind and space and time. Yet the raven seemed to be flying with purpose. Searching. Landing. Looking. No… Seeing. Then spreading its wings and taking to the air once again. The Queen's eyes followed its course, swooping over the rooftops, racing above the crowds with their boxes and carts, unloading ready for a day of presenting their wares. Her vantage point gave her a secrecy she enjoyed, not for the voyeuristic power but here she could observe their clear pride at showing their Queen their hard-wrought goods and foods before it misted over in a veil of nerves in her presence.

And then their eyes met.

Looking up at her. Piercing.

Beside a young boy in awe of his surroundings, a woman with jet black hair stood in the crowd alongside a laden cart. Not helping. Not moving. As if detached from the reality of the courtyard. Looking. Seeing. The Queen felt instantly uncomfortable, but not afraid. She was used to being scrutinised, observed like an object, but not analysed. The woman seemed to cock her head very slightly to one side. Her clothing was simple but well chosen, the cheapness of the fabric belying a knowledge of garment and fit. Yet it was not just her garb that stood her apart; she had an air of assuredness that the Queen only saw in those of high breeding or comfort in upper society. It was certainly not something she had expected to find amongst the bustle and straw of the courtyard. She was aware that the gaze had been held for far too long, but she could not look away.

"Ma'am."

A tentative voice from somewhere nearby.

"Ma'am?"

Within the room.

"Ma'am, if I could ju…"

"Yes! Yes…" snapped the Queen with a sharp inhale. Turning, she looked across the room at the bowed head of a serving girl. "What is it?" She realised her own haughtiness. "Sorry… Yes, Maryam, how can I help you?" The young maid tucked her flowing brunette hair behind her ear.

"The, um, the service cards for today's Festival of Provender… they are, ready."

"Thank you." The Queen smiled warmly. "I shall be down soon." The young serving girl nodded and backed her way to the doorway before disappearing into the shadowy corridor beyond. Watching her go, the monarch sighed. She loved the people, her people, and greatly appreciated these moments of connection and celebration, but the relentlessness of the traditions and ceremonies was tiresome. With a slow, drawn breath her gaze returned to the crowd from her viewpoint at the ornate window.

The raven-haired woman was gone. Many people flittered this way and that around the few remaining carts that had not been unloaded of their produce, ready for the stalls that had been temporarily set up in the banquet hall. The wagon from the tavern was not where it had been; the boy no longer gawking round in wonder. And the female with the piercing eyes, where was she now? The Queen breathed in, a tightening in her chest, a burning sensation in her hands. Here. She was here.

*   *   *

Tolva's saccharine smile dropped as the castle guard stood aside and she stepped beyond him. Having strode from the courtyard under the arches of the castle doorway, her heart had pulsed with the desire to see with her own eyes the sights and secrets of the inner rooms of the great, white building. She had dreamed of this chance for over a year, and she could not waste it now. Leaving Hopps to unload the produce from its carefully packed boxes, she had made the excuse of needing to find water and collected a discarded pewter jug before heading through a half-closed doorway. Beyond, the oak-panelled room with its imposing bookcases and moody landscape paintings had only served to whet her appetite further. Open doors became invitations and Tolva soaked up every decorative ornament, every hand-carved piece of furniture, the smells and sounds of rooms she had no right to be venturing into. Until, finally, a guard in perfectly steam-cleaned livery halted her.

"Madam, you are not permitted to be in this part of

the building." Despite the sternness of his voice, his eyes weakened at the coy look on the face of the diminutive lady in front of him. The intensity of her eyes made him look away.

"Oh, my good sir, I was merely looking for a little cool water… The closeness of the crowd was making me feel faint." Tolva toyed with the man who now shifted uneasily. Without lifting his head he pointed to his right.

"Down there. Second door. No, third… I'm not…" But he did not finish his sentence before shuffling away. The jug that had been so useful to her as a prop was cast aside on the corner of a decorative table. The banquet hall, with its assortment of offerings and wares, was an interesting sideshow, but now that she was inside the inner sanctums, the secrets of the castle were too tantalising to resist. Leaving the aromas and chatter of the market-style festival far behind, her footsteps made very little sound on the smooth flagstones as she passed through the dim castle corridor. She imagined catching glimpses of private chambers, with normal, everyday life taking place behind closed doors. She imagined standing atop one of the towers surveying the

lands of Fenwood, peering down on the people
scurrying about their humdrum lives. Imagined passing
the Queen in one of the candlelit corridors, taking in
her scent, smiling politely before heading to the hall to
sample the produce of her adoring public. Tolva
allowed herself the fantasy of power, running her
fingertips along the clammy walls, feeling the pulse of
the castle, Fenwood's beating heart.

Tolva had paused at several staircases, both up and
down, taking in the air that drifted from the floors and
corridors beyond. Sometimes musty, sometimes
fragranced, sometimes aromatic. Nearing the end of the
passageway, an innocuous set of steps dissolved beyond
the candles to the right, curling away, embracing the
ominous gloom. Crossing the cold floor, Tolva hovered
at the bottom step, listening to the darkness above.

"...I will not..."

"...how dare you..."

"...those are my people..."

Whispers on the breath of the air.

Despite never hearing them before, she knew the
voices. Steadying herself with a hand on the damp
stone, her delicate feet ascended the steps, merging her

shadow as she left the light behind her.

"…every time you degrade yourself with this charade…" A man's voice, thick with loathing, thick with drink, a rebuttal to the gathered strength of the female who kept her poise.

"Do not accompany me. In this state you reflect badly on…"

"On what?! On you? On the crown? Go on…"

"On yourself. On your family."

Tolva reached the top before the hand made contact with the face; her emergence into the light coming to the Queen's defence, her presence a shield to his wrath. The King, dressed clumsily in his finery, reeled, his arm wavering in the air. Rage foamed at the corners of his mouth. His eyes, blood-shot, struggled to focus on her features. Turning his focus back to his wife, he sneered.

"You're no queen," he spat, and flounced away in a flurry of robes.

The royal lady remained upright, stoic, but Tolva saw the flickering light reflecting off watering eyes.

"Thank you," muttered the Queen, rattled and embarrassed, but not prepared to let her regal front fall.

"Lucky I arrived when I did," returned Tolva. The

Queen nodded, but something in the air sensed that luck was not at play. She studied the face of the black-haired woman, the downward curve of her nose exaggerated in the dim, flickering candles.

"The courtyard. I saw you. Watching me," she began, addressing the obvious tension.

"Yes." Tolva remained aloof, and the moment hung in the air between them.

"You were with the carts. Do you work in the town?"

"I do." Tolva nodded. "At the tavern."

The conversation stopped. Finally the Queen took the lead again.

"Please, do head back down to the hall. I shall be there momentarily. Without my husband." A show of strength that Tolva nodded at in approval. Turning away from the unease, she took the first step down the slow-spiral staircase. But the Queen's voice caused her to stop.

"Do not mention this. Please. It is a private matter. Not one for public spectacle and idle gossip."

Tolva placed her hand on her heart and bowed her head before dropping again into the blackness.

*   *   *

She was aware of the green eyes tracking her movements as she made her way from table to table in the banqueting hall, sampling wares and exchanging pleasantries in her well-practised, queenly manner. She avoided the stall where the woman and the energetic child stood behind platters of wholesome, common fare. The event was a proclaimed success; the Queen felt such apprehension and discomfort, and as she beamed her final smiles before heading for the exit she was able to breathe a sigh of relief. Making her way back along the inner corridors, she paused by some of the more experienced staff, enquiring after the lady from the tavern.

"She's new to the town…"

"…came from no one knows where…"

"Name begins with T, I think… Tatiana?"

"…a bit strange… Don't say much."

Having gathered nothing of any use, the Queen said many a "fair night" and closed her chamber door.

Darkness had fallen long before a somewhat

surprised Ernest was summoned to the Queen's private room. Knocking as softly as he could, in case she had at last found sleep, the servant was bidden to enter. He found his mistress sat at her dressing table, but pots of ink and clay beakers of cut feathers had replaced the vials and ramekins of oils and creams. Two letters lay sealed on the desk, carefully positioned, as if the lady had arranged and rearranged them whilst considering something acutely. She looked up when he entered, and he thought her face to have lines of worry and deep thought.

"Ernest. I have a request for you. Something important." He nodded in understanding and she took the papers in her hands. "This letter" – holding the one in her left hand forward – "is for Janelle Dawn. I need him to reach out his long, spidery fingers in the cities for information on our new resident." In front of her, the man's face showed a flash of quizzical eyebrows but, again, nodded. She continued, holding out the other paper. "And this is for the Master of Guards. I want the girl brought to me in the morning of five days time. I should have heard some news by then."

"Yes, ma'am." His dependable hands took both

letters. He opened his mouth to ask the question that was at the forefront of his mind.

"No, Ernest, not this time." The Queen knew the look on his face. "I have made up my mind, and will not be swayed." With a final nod, the man made his way to the door and closed it smoothly behind him on his way out. In truth, she was unsure whether what she was doing was right, but the sensation she felt to her very core when this mystical woman was near could not be ignored; it would be safer to have her close, to have her within the inner sanctum. And, something more than this, the Queen knew she was significant. Something alive. Something fateful.

CHAPTER SIX

SERVICE AND DUTY

Tolva awoke to a castle guard at the door to the Oaks.
Whether due to the early hour or being sworn to
secrecy, he said very little, but the royal mark on the fine
paper he carried said it all. A summons. Searching his
face, she merely nodded and pulled on the short silver
coat she had laid out ready.

*   *   *

The iron-gilded bedroom door was open and Tolva
waited patiently, just as the lady-in-waiting had
instructed her to. Glancing back, she marvelled at how
close she had come those nights before, the
incongruous flight of stairs rising to a corridor which
housed the Queen's chamber. Or one of them. The
room did not look lived in; there were no piles of
clothes and even the pots and jars on the dressing table

appeared purposefully arranged. The figure at the dresser was instantly recognisable, facing the mirror, back to the door, brushing her long, shining, whitening hair, slowly. Tolva remained in place, not crossing the battle line at the door, hands clasped behind her back, determined not to break first.

The stand-off lasted some minutes.

"Can you plait hair?" The Queen's question was blunt, without turning or looking toward the waiting individual she knew was in the doorway. The reply was quiet, controlled.

"I can, my lady."

The seated lady glanced back momentarily at Tolva in the doorway before carefully choosing her words. "You are well travelled, I hear. I can assume you have experience of materials and garments. Perhaps even fashions from afar?"

"I do, my lady." Tolva knew this was not a question about clothing, and she understood that the Queen had some knowledge of her past. Silence again followed, but with a slow, reluctant acceptance.

"Can you be trusted to be loyal and true in public engagements?" the Queen asked. Tolva nodded, not in reply but in understanding of what was happening.

"I can be welcoming and charmingly distant where appropriate."

A hint of a smile touched the corners of the royal lips. The level of awareness in the slender woman standing by the door was far beyond that of the girls currently in her service. But there was something deeper, darker even. The Queen paused her methodical brushing.

"And what else can you do?" Her gaze pierced the mirror, scrutinising the lowered head in the doorway. The question was a challenge.

"Many things…" Tolva's response was guarded. "I can serve in a number of ways, your Grace." She raised her head and met the Queen's eyes in the large, ornate-framed reflective glass. The lingered look signed an unwritten contract.

"There are white dresses, gowns and tunics in the servants' quarters." The royal woman returned to brushing.

When the Queen glanced back, the enigmatic woman had gone and the doorway was clear. Setting down the brush, she let out a trapped breath. Tolva. Tolva. She had practised the conversation several times so as not to seem weak. In truth, she was afraid of Tolva, of the strength within her, and she felt trust and something... something she could not understand.

*　　　*　　　*

Several girls shuffled in and out of a large dressing room filled with white dresses, smocks and aprons. The majority of them ignored the avian figure waiting patiently at the doorway, some because they were busy attending to their morning tasks whilst others felt intimidated by her intensity. A bold, clipped voice summoned her from somewhere within the folds and fabrics of the room.

"Girl? Yes, you by the door – new one. Come here."

Tolva stepped through the doorway and looked around her. White. A lot of white. And there between the racks and dresses was a large, rounded woman whose apron strings cut into her billowing body like string in soft dough; her cropped hair more brilliant than the garments around her.

"Name?" Tolva's face clearly showed her surprise at

the bluntness. "Your name?" the woman pressed, sarcastically. "You have one? Oh the Gods, you're not another of these vacuous saps our beloved Queen keeps sending to me…"

"Tolva," the word interjected as a pointed response.

"Oh, she speaks." The women studied each other for a moment. "Tolva…" The dressing-lady smiled to herself, a private joke from years of experience. "Tolva… Of course it is…" Tolva almost snapped but maintained her dignity and composure; the dresser watched her, wanting the challenge, reading the fire in Tolva's eyes. With a wry smile, she began holding up items of clothing toward the new serving girl, who shook her head without really looking at the items.

"Is there a problem here?" The doughy face sighed, both enjoying and tired of the challenge.

"Yes." Tolva narrowed her eyes. "Do you have anything other than white?".

Eight ladies-in-waiting lined up in a breezy lower ground corridor, backs to the wall as a severe, moustachioed man looked over the top of a rounded eye-glass, inspecting, scrutinising, judging. Tolva's beady eyes quietly watched him. His shoulders, encased in a purple velvet jacket, barely moved as he walked with his toes pointing before he stepped. Finally, he stopped alongside a slender-faced red-haired girl.

"Florence, today you shall be on cloth duty." She tried not to show it but her eyes read disappointment, and she nodded with silent compliance. He continued down the line, coming to a pause three maids further along. "Holly. For you, linens." Tolva assumed she would be last, but to her surprise she was next on the precise man's order of services. "Tolva. New girl." He gave her another look up and down.

"Yes, si…"

"No no, we don't need to talk. First day, silverware. Begin in the library. Marie will show you the way. Tomms will be there." And he moved on.

The division of tasks for the day was the same each morning and afternoon, but the task itself would differ. When they were off-service some of the girls would bemoan their distributed activity and talk vehemently about their most or least favourite tasks. Tolva remained quiet. They had none of them experienced a life beyond the comfort of the castle walls, never stooped so low in order to survive. She found it difficult to speak to her fellow serving ladies; she knew they did not like her, thinking her arrogant and aloof, but she did not care. She fed off the potency of the castle, observed and learned, and at the end of each day she lay in bed and processed everything, storing it for when it would be needed.

The view from the small square window looked out over the herb garden, sprawling away on the lower ground floor of the castle lands. Tolva wiped the morning condensation from the glass pane, smiling to herself at the advancement in her situation. Her new quarters were small but clean, sparse but comfy; the bed covers were washed, soft, and there were always clean clothes to wear. But more than that, the whole room did not smell of beer and grease. Other bedrooms cascaded off to the left and right, and whilst she did not socialise with the other serving girls, there was never a shortage of company when needed. She would be forever grateful to Roker for the rope that had been thrown for her to cling on to, to build stability from, but the inn had only ever been a means to an end. Her abilities would be needed here.

There was variety in her new life, and fruitful

opportunities. Some days Tolva was castle-bound, attending to the Queen's needs; folding gowns and sheets rather than drying cups and mopping tables. On other days there would be a ceremony or celebration to prepare for; these were plentiful and revered by all. Tolva found these occasions bizarre, quaint even, but would make herself useful in whatever she was asked: folding hundreds of dinner-cloths; arranging flowers in ceramic pots; dusting and cleaning in endless, sprawling rooms that seemed to see very little, if any, use. Very rarely was she part of the ceremony itself. Market days were her favourite; aiding and informing the Queen's closest advisors on creams and jewellery and fabrics, or having time to herself to understand Fenwood, what the land offered, local names and faces. Remembering and recording.

Despite being in the Queen's service, she did not spend much time in her presence, and Tolva could not help but think this was not an accident. Something happening in another room; a need for Tolva to collect items from the town; calling for aid from another servant. Tolva would show no reaction. She could take her time.

Despite her indifference towards her colleagues and seniors, respect grew for Tolva through her initiative and thoroughness. There was a confidence, a self-assuredness, in the quiet way she went about her tasks. She never took nor needed advice. She needed no surety or gratification from her so-called superiors, and certainly the timid girls, who almost cowered in her presence, seldom built up the courage to speak to her. Yet her manner was easy-going and calm; children and lower-ranking servants found her gracious, comforting, unpretentious. And these relationships became important to her.

'You'll never guess who I saw out in the courtyard with the stable hand last night...'

'That slovenly Mira has been stealing venison again...'

'I hear the King was out in the middle-night again of late... No, not at The Oaks, at that horrible drinking hole under the Eastern boughs...'

'Now I know she don't eat meat, but I seen her pulling the fat off bacon and shovelling it in...'

'Apparently the Queen has asked for more of those tablets again – you know, the ones to help with getting pregnant...'

Tolva would nod, raise eyebrows, smile, but never

comment or judge. Merely listened, remembered. She thrived off the scraps and morsels of information that she could gather, storing it up from her 'little ones'; never for malevolence, but for influence. What the raven did not see, other 'birds' in the physically impenetrable, secretive castle could.

*   *   *

The morning struggled to clear the darkness of the night before as heavy rainclouds suffocated the sun. Rain droplets swirled viscously on the wind that bore on it the rumour of chaos and distant threat of wolf howls. Inside the walls, the castle grumbled in dampened discontent. The Master of Ceremonies and Services had been slow to wake, using the grey mist as an excuse to pull the duvet higher and hide from the grim morn. Tolva breakfasted alone, peeling her boiled egg to the accompanying rapid beat of rain on the scullery window. When she finished, only a few of the maids had appeared, and even the corridors had an eerie slumbering silence. Purposefully, she allowed her feet to make a wrong turn at the servants' chambers, snaking her way up a narrow tower staircase to the Royal Ceremonial bedroom, where the regal figure often readied herself for the day. Approaching carefully, the door was closed and the room dormant. Tolva paused and looked up and down the wider passageway, often a hive of activity, but this morning… nothing. Satisfied that she was alone, she placed a thin, bony hand against the cold wall and closed her eyes. Controlled her breathing. Concentrated. And there it was: the sound of voices.

As Tolva rounded the corner she realised where she was and set her sights on the shaft of light that spilled from a doorway halfway down the passage. The voices got louder as she got closer, so she slowed her pace, coming to a stop by the hinges of the oak door that stood open by just a fraction. Inside, the Queen spoke in hushed tones, but frustration had caused her to lose control at the volume at which she was speaking.

"It sounds like you are saying it is my fault."

"No, ma'am, not at all—" the second voice floundered.

"I have tried everything!" the Queen cut in, the words carried with anger and sadness. "Everything you have said…"

"I know."

"So it is YOUR fault! Your fault I have no heir. Your fault the kingdom will falter." The words were irrational, panicked.

"Ma'am…"

"No! Go. Get out. Leave. Leave me, a barren crone…"

The door suddenly flew open and the unrecognised figure stumbled into the dark behind Tolva.

"I cannot go through this again!" shrieked the Queen, clearly holding back tears, revealing herself in the open door frame. The other woman, holding a listening device, searching for breath, ran away down the corridor. Tolva observed the royal face in front of her, desperate and shocked at having been overheard.

"I'm sorry, ma'am, I did not mean to hear that." Tolva dropped her head through genuine shame at having listened.

"No," came the embarrassed reply, "I should not have said… what I said…aloud…" Now conscious of further prying eyes and ears, they slipped back into the chamber. Their closeness was uncomfortable, Tolva hovering by the door with an awareness that she had overstepped a boundary. The eyes of the two women met across the room. An unspoken understanding passed between them. A knowing. The Queen seemed to be searching for words that she did not know if she wanted to find, and subconsciously her hands ran over her stomach. The look of acceptance dwindled to awkwardness. Tolva held the gaze for a beat and turned to leave.

"You're a witch, aren't you."

The bluntness caught Tolva off guard. It was a statement rather than a question. She had been through so much to deny and escape it. Slowly, she turned back and re-met the Queen's scrutinising eyes.

"No. Well…" She had never tried to explain it before. "Not in the way you think." Tolva took a step forward, but the Queen held her position on the other side of the bed. She expected the sovereign to say something but the older lady held her calm and waited before an almost proud admittance.

"I sensed it. When I saw you. Something… A presence. A power." Tolva kept a straight expression on her face, practised in servitude, unblinking, even as she felt a faint tug at the corners of her mouth. "I had you followed." Still the monarch did not turn and the smile edged onto Tolva's face, of both shock and admiration. "This... power, what is it?" the Queen pressed.

"I can... do certain things. Abilities, perhaps." Again, she paused, but the Queen showed no sign of emotion. Now Tolva felt vulnerable. "I have always been able to sense things. To feel the world around me... It's hard to explain. A bond with the natural world. I can feel what it feels, see what it sees—"

"The raven," interrupted the Queen.

"Yes, like with the raven." Tolva watched as the lady nodded, a private motion of confirmation. "I don't know, perhaps you'd call it an old form of magic." The Queen's face now looked through Tolva, beyond her, as if contemplating what opportunity this could provide. Tolva sat slowly on a velveteen stool, unsure of how the Queen would react.

"Have you always had this... these abilities? Were you born with it?" A question, but no eye contact.

"Yes, but it took me many years to understand it. Not that I fully understand it now."

"Did someone help you?" The question was abrupt,

like someone searching for information.

"Yes…" Tolva paused, her heartbeat noticeable in her chest. "Yes," she repeated, "my mother. She was Gifted. But people scorned her." At this Tolva fell silent and the Queen, sensing genuine emotion, looked over at the black-haired lady.

"They burned her." Tolva's face hardened. "And I refuse to surrender to the same fate."

Once again, there was an understanding between the two women, even admiration. And suddenly Tolva realised that what the independent, strong lady in front of her was struggling with was coming to terms with where the conversation was now inevitably heading. This time, when their eyes met, she felt the Queen's gaze searching her. Controlling her breathing. Wrestling with self-control. All those instances of keeping this mystical creature at arm's length, but within sight. The hesitation to trust. Opening the doors to chaos.

"You can help me, can't you." Statement, not a question.

Tolva nodded, calmly but confidently. "Yes. Yes, I believe I can."

The two women spoke long into the night.

CHAPTER SEVEN
THE WILD

The Queen remembered the passage through the Oaken Ring from when she was a girl. She had trodden it many times, when she dreamed of a life beyond tradition and expectations, before giving in to the duties and luxuries that her life as a princess had expected of her. In many ways she now held some of the excitement and trepidation as the girl dressed in expensive clothes had done when she stole from her life for an adventure in the Outlands, carrying only a bag jumbled with food and leftovers, her viewing glass and, secretly, a soft stuffed rabbit with one ear and worn-down eyes. But now, as the moon sang its loudest, the bag slung over her shoulder jangled and clacked with items Tolva had carefully written down to help her with the ritual. The branches parted easily with a brush of her hand, as they had done so many years ago. The breeze through the leaves seemed like a sigh, a gladness.

Her leather-soled shoes, lovingly bestowed upon her by Tanner who ran the leather stall at the market (she was unsure whether this was his real name or a nickname, whether he chose the vocation or it chose him), trod the still-grassed path that she had been assured would be there. She looked ahead for a tree in the shape of a 'Y' with leaves darker than its brothers and sisters. The gathering dusk made identifying hues of leaves tricky, but before long the sign that she had been looking for rose purposefully at a fork in the path. Rummaging in her cloth bag, the Queen pulled out a small glass vial. In the darkening light the liquid that swirled within the glass looked dark blue. Bending, she poured the thin liquor at the base of the tree where its slender trunk joined the earth. There it lingered, pooled, for some time, before sinking through the moss and soil in one. Peering down the left-hand path, she slung the light-canvas bag back over her shoulder and turned her attention to the right-hand fork. Brambles began to creep in at ankle height but Tolva had informed her clearly of the route. With a last glance back in the direction of the forest edges, the regal figure stepped over a spiked, groping arm and watched the tendrils of bushes close her in. Her purpose set. Her resolve hardened. She allowed the forest to take her.

*   *   *

High above, from the large decorative chamber window, Tolva watched the distant silver-haired shape scurry with a nervous excitement from the cover of oaken safety to the unknown of the forest fringes. The quill with which she had written directions and items still sat in its pot of ink in front of her on the congested desk. She smiled, but not due to any sense of power; a warmth spread through her veins. Remaining at the window, Tolva waited until the Queen had disappeared from view beneath the bowers and boughs. She had done what she could to help and the feeling that flowed through her now was… pride? Satisfaction? Inner peace?

As she mulled over this new sensation, a shadow within broke the light. A negative presence. Without turning, Tolva spoke.

"The Queen is engaged and cannot take any more visitations tonight."

The midwife paused in the doorway, terrified but determined. She took tentative step forward.

"I have cared for her for years and…"

"…and look what good it has done her." At that, Tolva turned. The midwife faltered and Tolva continued to press. "If you wish I can tell the Queen you called by?" The tone of her voice already held the confidence of triumph. Yet the shorter, dumpier opponent rallied.

"You do not care for her. You are slow poison. You just want to feel—"

The word 'poison' stung Tolva. "I care so much that I actually act, get things done," she cut across. "What have you done?" She had been bitten. "I mean, actually done? Yes, you have soothed and pandered" – she began to pace threateningly toward the retreating midwife, her rage rising from her stomach to her tongue – "but what have you done for her? What have you given her? She wants a child. You cannot give her that." Any battle of wills became an onslaught.

"I… I have tried to…"

"You have failed." It was blunt, imposing. "That is what you have done. Failed. Time and time again." She towered over the midwife now, berating her. "I do not need the Queen to feel power. I am more powerful than she will ever be…" But she stopped herself, aware of the arrogance that now fell freely from her forked tongue. Beneath her, the cowering woman waited for the next volley, a crushing blow. It never came. Seeing the hesitation, the midwife backed away, muttering.

"You are a beast. Vicious. A ravenous wolf…"

The door slammed shut in safety. Tolva breathed deeply, quenching her rage. She ran her hands over her eyes, squeezing them shut. Needing the air, she moved back to the window and looked out over the falling night. It calmed her. Glancing down at the bottles and dishes, she knew she could reject them all. The world outside these walls was remedy enough, and if anything could work for the Queen, then the forest would provide.

Then, without warning, the shadow again. Tolva sensed it with a burning heat and turned, expecting the return of the midwife.

"I thought I made it cl…"

The King's unfocussed eyes and imposing frame filled the doorway. He had on a silken nightshirt, fine cloth and clearly expensive, but the impact was marred by the brown ale stains that drizzled down the front.

"Where is she?" he pressed, coldly. Not looking directly at the black-haired woman in front of him, Vilius wiped spittle from his greying beard. Tolva exhaled pointedly, a warning hiss from an animal under threat.

"Out," she spat.

The huge, guttural laugh that issued forth from the King disarmed her through shock. She felt vulnerable. He lurched his body from its leaning position and into the room.

"Out? She is never out! Her whole life exists here!" This time his sleeve sufficed to blockade the frothing spit that clung to his wiry chin hair. "You've got spirit, I'll give you that. And brash confidence. But you're no different from the other wenches that flit around her. Breakable." He sat, collapsed, on the edge of the bed, bounced up and down for a moment like a child, gazed up at the tapestries. "That one's new," he chuckled.

A silence descended in the room. Tolva fidgeted uncomfortably by the window, eyeing the open door across the room.

"Sir, I apologise, but I need to…"

"Oh, 'sir' is it now?" he mocked, turning toward her. His eyes settled on her face, studying her as his mind attempted to drunkenly recall moments and memories. Then, with an unsettling look, his gaze moved down her body. "I know you." A leering grin twitched in the corners of his mouth. "The new one. But you think you know it all." Licked his lips. "Low born, clearly. Think you're better than us. I've seen you. Think you can do it all."

Tolva could not read the smile that wrinkled his face.

"I just want her to be happy." Pause. "And successful. To use her power to—"

"Her power?!" There was that laugh again, filled with knowing and derision. "I made her who she is!" His voice had changed, rising with deep-seated rage and bitterness. "And now I am shunned, ignored. A leper. A dirty rumour. All because I could not… cannot… put a baby in her belly." He was frothing again, wallowing in drink and pity. Tolva furtively glanced to the open doorway. "You and your fellow little chattering bitches, whispering lies and meddling… turning her—"

Tolva bolted for the door. Catching Vilius off guard,

the movement stopping him mid rant. She was light and nimble, and in her wits. There was no way she could fight and had seen her opportunity to flee, the primal instinct of protection. But she had misjudged him, even in his liquor. A muscular arm shot out, almost as she passed him, and took a firm hold of her wrist, upsetting her balance; before she could regain her posture, he was rising and his opposing hand was around her throat. Tolva choked and wheezed, but any hope of screaming immediately left her, crushed under the threat of strangulation.

"Flying so soon, little bird?"

She was almost lifted as he stood, her toes tapping and scraping frantically at the stone floor. Her vision fizzed and blurred. Head pounding. Then she was airborne, flying, crashing to the mattress. Tolva was dazed, blood rushing to her brain. She was aware of his weight bearing down upon her body even as her sight was returning from blurred shadows. Then a savage, sharp, heavy strike to the face.

Black circles.

Leaden body.

Rough hands.

Stop.

Nothingness.

*   *   *

The wolf took to its heels. Bounding through the dense forest at night, her eyes adjusted to the stifling darkness. She sniffed the air as she accelerated over jutting roots and slid her way under low-hanging bows. Inclining her head to the direction she knew her children to be in, she let out a high howl, a call that warned of danger; it echoed through the woodland and ran in panicked whispers along branches. The ground beneath her thudding paws pulsated with a rhythm of impending chaos, rousing the core of the trees and bushes, the wind echoing a chorus of violence to the moon. From afar, an answering call, followed by a second, both safe and alert. A third? Her pace slowed, again taking note of the scents on the air. Two short searching, guttural growls. Stopping momentarily at the top of a slope, she held high her head in hope of a returning cry, but as none came she descended the shifting, debris slope until her feet dampened at the edges of a large, sheltered body of water.

The pool that stretched out before her was silent, still, protected from the rumour of oncoming turmoil by trees and something that the wolf could not place. She had been here many times, tasted the water, felt its sleeping majesty, but today there was an ominous closeness. Her fur bristled and her back arched, vigilant to the unknown fear. Moving under the drooping arms of the trees, she traced the edge of the water, somehow not creating ripples with her movement. The further banks of the water's edge on the opposite side opened up as she rounded the curves and inlets of the pool. And that's when she saw it. Her mother's senses wrenching a strangled groan from her throat. A pile of fur and twisted features and matted blood. The groan in her throat became a growl, before she lifted her head and unleashed a full-blooded cry.

*   *   *

Her body was numb. Laying in the gathering dark she hoped and begged for death. Her vision was broken, through disorientation and brutality and night. Alone on the bed, she felt a weight pressing on her chest. Memory. An angel. A raven. A wolf. Mustering all the strength she could, Tolva rolled onto her side, allowing the stinging bile to empty from her mouth onto the sheets beside her and splatting onto the floor. From somewhere deep within her, a voice flared up, a raging infernal spirit:

'Get up. Get out.'

*　　　*　　　*

She watched as they dragged him away. Her children, as gently as they could, took their brother to the family burial ground, deep in the heart of the forest. She stood tall, proud, composed. Wolf mother. But inside her heart was breaking. She had lost children before to the wild, from previous litters, and it never got easier. Slowly, she followed the mournful procession, taking in the last smells of her son, dragging her nose on the ground. Her eldest children would prepare the body now, and she would prepare the family for what the forest foretold was coming.

CHAPTER EIGHT
MOTHERHOOD

Tolva's stomach rolled, turned and she heaved for the fourth time. There was nothing left but retching foam that hung in strands from her wounded lip. The force of the hacking throbbed in her bruised and swollen face. Breathing in, the room reeked of vomit and mould. She had stumbled, unseeing, unknowing, from the chamber, fumbling along corridors and stumbling down staircases, until she had collapsed into an unlocked room somewhere in the stale basement of the castle. Blood-strewn clothes now scattered the floor, in and around the trails of sick that still hung in thin strands from her lips. Her hair was wet with sweat and blood. Never had she felt so helpless. She was a survivor, a warrior, but now her tears fell in free-flowing torrents and her inflamed throat choked with guttural cries from her very core.

*   *   *

The Queen knew not how but the trees had guided her, just as Tolva had assured her they would; branches bent, beckoned, ushered, leading her to a leaf-veiled clearing. The foliage parted with ease at a gentle, inquisitive push.

She stepped forward into a small glade with soft grass underfoot, but ahead she could see that this gave way to shingled sand, sloping down to a still mirror of water. Around the silent pool, old trees formed a protective enclosure, shielding the waters from unwanted interference, prying eyes, preserving its natural magic. The Queen could sense its power emanating all around its primal beauty and elegance. She had never been particularly spiritual, but here she could sense the hands of the Gods. She allowed her feet to break the stillness of the water. Ripples cascaded across the surface, gliding to the far banks, swaying the water ferns and drifting the lilies. The pool was cool to touch, but not cold. She inhaled, paused, and exhaled. She could do this.

The pool watched and waited. It had known that a figure of importance was imminent, but time had dulled its senses. The waters, ever still, had sparkled once with vigour and energy, but had fallen into dormancy. Now something stirred. A deep breath, all round.

When it had been explained to her back in the confines of the chamber, the ritual had seemed complicated and the Queen had asked Tolva to write it down. However, now she was here and all the artefacts were lined up on the bank it all felt right and, somehow, natural. Firstly, taking the wrapped velvet parcel carefully in her hand, she dug a shallow hole in the earth and, having placed the small object in the bottom, covered it back over with the excavated dirt. She had not wanted to ask what was inside, but as she held it in her hand it felt like many tiny bones. Brushing off her hands, unaccustomed as they were to dirt since her teenage years, she next took up the cylindrical glass vial. Holding it up to the glittering moonlight, the liquid inside gave off a deep crimson lustre. There was something viscous about the contents, and she knew what it was even without opening the container. Her fingers closed around it as her linen dress lifted easily over her head. She had thought this would be the most awkward part of the ritual, but now, standing naked at the water's edge, she felt a freedom seldom experienced before. Again, she breathed deeply. The breeze whispered its reassurance. With a gentle 'pop', the small bottle opened; the Queen carefully poured the oozing liquid onto two fingers and, as instructed, smeared it over her stomach. Several times she did this in the symbol Tolva had shown her. Despite the uncertainty she felt, her determination willed her on. She had nothing to lose.

The cold water of the pool felt soft around her ankles, like a gentle coaxing. Red droplets fell from her fingertips to the water and were absorbed into its mystical depths. Looking around, she understood that here she was no queen, that the pool and the trees and the air loved and accepted her for being a woman. And that maybe, just maybe, they would want her to be a mother. As she waded forward, the waters of the pool rose up her legs and her nakedness, reaching her stomach. She gasped in expectancy of some sensation, but felt nothing but the shock of the temperature. Soon, finding herself near the centre of the sheltered mere, it covered her torso, her breasts. Letting the silent waters caress her shoulders, the Queen gave herself to the natural world.

* * *

Tolva regained consciousness. A blood-stain on the floor where her face had been showed that she had lain, frozen in position, for some time. For a moment she could not remember what had happened, how she was so torn and battered. The sound of fire crackled in her ears and her skin stung from flames unseen. Screams and howls echoed around her. An acrid taste of burning prickled her tongue. Tolva tried to raise her hand to her face but she could not tell if the wetness at her fingertips was cold, damp stone or the flesh from her cheeks melting away to the touch.

"You'll burn for this…" she mumbled, cracked lips barely parting. Tolva lost consciousness.

* * *

For some time she sat on the bank, wrapped in a blanket, gazing out across the glassy surface as it reflected the luminescence of the moon. Her mind raced with a thousand questions. Here she had the freedom to wonder. She understood why Tolva had told her to come here, and even some understanding of her abilities. Fenwood had always had a connection with the natural world around it, but here there was an almost tangible symbiosis between the waters, the wind, the strong but gentle arms of the trees. Under the hand-crafted blanket, her hand rested on her stomach. She imagined that the sensation of nervous excitement was the beginning of new life. It would be a miracle. She smiled; at her age, people really would see it as a miracle. But they would welcome an heir. And for her... The Queen swallowed the tears that fought to fall. For her, there would be new meaning. A void in her life fulfilled. Love.

*   *   *

From somewhere she heard the rush of thousands of voices. The stone room became a hut of mud, the sound of praying and crying and laughing and shouting all at once swam through her mind, faces contorted into grotesque visions of features, eyes and mouths rolling, black porcelain eyes unblinking but not seeing. Silence.

Panting of breath. A single beast hurtling across a forest floor. An animal. A boy. With a wolf's face. Every time his knuckles crashed the ground beneath him, the leaves and twigs and stones threw up splashes of deep, crimson blood. Tolva cried out, clutching her stomach. And wept. Each tear draining away the little life she had left.

*　　　*　　　*

Bag slung over her shoulder, the silver-haired lady felt renewed energy flowing through her and picked her way over stumps and round trunks to the back of the pool. Here, years ago, somebody had dug stone slabs into the steep embankment. Hitching her dress, she confidently strode up, brushing off the scuff on her knee and scrape on her shin from a sharp edge. There was a lightness in her step as the path followed a field, illuminated in the moonlight. Pausing, she was momentarily transfixed by the maturing shafts of corn swaying, dancing in the silver light. She pictured children running with abandon through the maze of stalks, laughing with glee. 'Maybe, one day, my child…' she allowed herself to ponder, before shifting the weight of her bag on her shoulder and bounding on.

The steep uphill climb brought her through dense undergrowth and untrodden walkways to a muddied track littered with stone. To her right there appeared to be a clearing which, as she followed, led the Queen to a crossroads. The Crossroads. Memories flooded back of adventures from a time long ago, when she had not the responsibilities and cares and worries that had built as years had gone by. Standing in the middle, turning in a slow circle, she took in this central entrance route to the realm. Her realm. Her people. And suddenly pride swelled in her heart.

"My people," she muttered. Looking up at the signpost she saw the arm that pointed to Fenwood, but she already knew the way to go.

The town had never looked so beautiful to her regal eyes as it did under the new moon. Light danced off fresh straw, singing songs of sleep and harmony. The wood of the houses, dampening in the night air, smelt like an untouched forest. Moving through the empty streets, the Queen's footsteps made no sound. She felt no fear, only quiet wonder. Being able to pass through the labyrinthian passages and thoroughfares unrecognised and uninterrupted. Spreading her arms, she let her fingers touch the textures and craftsmanship, feeling again her connection with her home.

Rising from behind the undulating path, the castle looked a pinnacle of grandeur and ceremony. She knew and understood its importance, the role that it played for the town and people, but, as beautiful as its white walls were, it remained a necessity in her reinvigorated vision. The hour had grown so late that servants and workers were abed. Somewhere in a distant corridor the 'tap tap tap' of a night guard's staff on the flagstones could be heard. Without conscious thought, the Queen made her way to the tower steps and up toward the bed chamber, hoping Tolva would be there to hear about the ritual. Excitedly, she swung open the door. An eerie silence. A dishevelled bed. A torn tapestry. Droplets of blood on the stone floor.

From the window, out in the forest, a wolf howled.

CHAPTER NINE
THE SAVIOUR

Weylin's cart trundled along the uneven stone path, expertly stacked with logs that did not fall, even when the wooden frame itself threatened to topple. Before reaching the main doors, he veered to the side, taking a narrow track that followed the outside walls of the castle. His thick, trunk-like arms strained at the weight of the cargo but his grizzled face showed no outward signs of effort. His head and face of full, curled, greying hair and weather-worn, brown hide cloak were a frequent sight in and around the castle and town, even though his dwelling sat on the borders of the forest. He was not in the service of the royal family, but his forestry and hunting skills were utilised for feasting and heating the large rooms of the stone structure. He was kind yet formidable, strong both in body and will.

The path led some way along the castle border walls to a small oak door. Weylin's large, rugged hand knocked gently, the sound heavy in the internal courtyard beyond. The door was creaked open by seemingly invisible hands and the burly forester ducked under the low door frame to enter the castle grounds. He was polite and warm with those castle-hands who spoke to him or he happened to make eye contact with, but otherwise he did not feel the need to make 'chit chat'. He knew his task, he knew his route.

"Weylin! You bring fair warm air with you!" came a call from a stable.

"Aye, it's been a fine few days," he replied, inclining his head but not slowing his pace.

"Lock up your'n daughters, handsome outlanders abound!" joked another.

"More like your mothers!" he quipped in reply, advancing to the far end of the avenue, undoing the latch on a further ageing wooden door and entering a smaller quad. It seemed a dead end, but lifting a slate covering in the far corner (half-disguised as a flagstone) revealed a long, easing set of steps, themselves sloped, that gave entrance to a lower storage area of the castle itself. Weylin screwed up his nose at the musty smell that escaped and began to lower himself and his laden cart into the bowels of the great, white structure.

The lower corridors and basements were lit by a combination of light tunnels by day and flaming torches by night. The truck rattled along the irregular floor, noise reverberating around the corridor walls, breaking the decaying silence. He looked from left to right at the doors as he passed, knowing the usual storerooms where he deposited logs but wondering how often anyone visited these subterranean antechambers of the royal building.

A disparity caught his eye. A door, open, that never was. Instinctively he looked around but shadows in the corridor swallowed up any clarity of sight. He could hear soft breath from within so carefully picked his way forward and positioned himself with a steadying hand on the door frame. Craning his neck, he peered in. The room was sparse but stifling. A girl. No. A woman, with black hair. Shaking. Whimpering. Staring. Holding herself in the stifling darkness of a storeroom.

"Miss? Miss? Are you alright?" Then all at once he seemed to notice her swollen and bruised face, the blood-strewn soft paper on the floor. Without hesitation, Weylin let the handle of his cart hit the ground with an echoing thud and was at the lady's side in three strides. Tenderly, he knelt beside her.

"Miss, what has happened?" No answer. She was clearly drifting somewhere between consciousness and senseless paralysis, eyes rolling back in her head. The violence of the scene incapacitated Weylin. He almost placed his hand on her knee to gain some interaction, but the blood between her thighs made him freeze. Looking up at the bruised face, her one usable eye was on him but looking through, unseeing; he had seen the look of startled panic before in traumatised animals. And he knew she could not stay here, for her own health and, possibly, safety. Something had attacked her and left her to die. They could return. Hastily grabbing a hessian sheet from a shelf, Weylin threw it around her fragile shoulders. She fell forward in a fitful collapse and he caught her, gathering her trembling body into his arms and lifted her as easily as he would a newborn fawn.

The corridors maintained their macabre slumber, his thudding bootsteps a sudden, hurried heartbeat as he carried the frail creature from the confines of the castle and up the sloping platforms to the emerging morning light. Back through the doorways he moved, able to maintain the lightness of his load with one arm as he worked door catches. He managed to pass through four interior lawns and courtyards before he was confronted by intrigued expressions: gardeners, whittlers, grinders and cleaners who lifted their ground-facing heads at the bulking intrusion.

"What're ye carrying there, Weylin?" came a coarse holler.

"Do not you fear, we warn't tell on ye," chuckled a crone, lubricating a mortar with her spit. Weylin merely grunted and nodded. Without breaking stride, he lurched on, pulling the sack-cloth down so as to not expose a dainty foot. The Gods favoured him that night as he met no other company in the castle grounds and, taking the lesser travelled paths around the dwellings, passed no figure in the town. By the time he reached the woodland edge, the form in his arms was deathly pale and blood stained his arms and overshirt. Passing under the hanging boughs, the forest held its breath and opened up the path before the woodsman.

His home, built by his own calloused hands, sat in a clearing and called out with faint hope as he glimpsed it through the foliage. By now, the load in his arms was a dead weight, arm hanging limp to the side and skin so white it was almost translucent. His heavy boots opened the door with a thud and he crossed the living space with great strides. Laying the body down on his bed, he feared she was dead. With surprising softness, he laid a tender hand on her side and felt the ever so faint rise and tremor of her ribs. Still alive. Just. He had cared for injured and wounded animals before, but this…

That night he bathed and dressed any wounds he could whilst she drifted in and out of fevered sleep. Being careful to maintain her decency, he cleaned off any blood that had begun to dry on her skin. Knowing that he had done what he could to aid her physical ailments, he boiled his pine remedy with water and allowed the aroma-heavy steam to drift in the air and ease in through her punctuated breathing. Finally, pulling up a chair, he settled himself in to watch over her; her breathing calmed as dawn kissed goodbye to another night, bringing in the daylight and new hope. Having stirred and fretted the day at her bedside, and with a renewed confidence that she would survive her injuries, Weylin left the hut to make his nightly rounds.

Owls sang in high branches and the wolves cried out to the moon.

When he returned, she had gone.

He looked for her when he delivered more wood, game and hide to the castle. Having retrieved his cart, he searched the grounds in case she had gone back, but only his own fading footprints could be traced. He returned time and time again; workers noticed an increase in his visits, but he offered no reason as to why.

He looked for her on his forays to Fenwood market where he showed little interest in the wares on display or the people who called out to him. He studied the faces and the gaps in the crowds, looking for her distinctive features or slight frame. But nothing.

He looked for her as he walked the paths of the forest, knowing beyond hope that she would not be there. Perhaps she had come to look for him, to see him, to thank him, but knew in his heart that she would not.

For days.

Weeks.

Months.

*   *   *

The Queen sat nervously on the edge of the bed, her hands clenching and unclenching the quilted covers. From behind the tapestry to her right, the hidden doors were open and the slow-growing crescendo of the gathering crowd outside could be heard. There had been a slow trickle of guests arriving throughout the morning as the news had gossiped along the weaving streets of Fenwood. They had come in families and small groups to find out what the castle needed to tell, and thus the crowd had grown. As a result, the Queen's anxiety had risen.

"Ma'am," ventured Ernest, hovering near an alcove, beginning to rub his thumb and forefinger together in a sign of controlled nervousness. The Queen did not raise her head as she shook it gently.

"I cannot…" she began, but the servant crossed the room swiftly and knelt at her side.

"Ma'am, if I may…" – he took her hands together in his – "the people will only love you more. This is strength."

"I know, Ernest, but…"

"No, Ma'am, no 'buts'." He stood, maintaining the hold on her hands. "Come, I will be here." Helping the lady to her feet, he marvelled to see how she straightened her back and raised her chin, finding again the poise with which she held herself for her people. Obligingly, he held back the tapestry curtain for her and she stepped out onto the balcony, adorned in a linen dress which exposed the secret that she had held through recent missed appointments and ceremonial absences. The hush of the crowd was broken by the gasps and cheers of realisation. The Queen was with child.

CHAPTER TEN

ACCEPTANCE AND REJECTION

The raven had not been seen in the skies above Fenwood for some time. Those who noted its absence assumed it found a suitable nested home in the woods outside of the Oaken Ring boundary. That, or the wolves had finally caught up with it. But it had, in fact, not left the castle. It had sheltered itself away, wrapped protectively in its own feathers, not wanting to be seen and not wanting to see.

*　　*　　*

The announcement of the royal pregnancy, an heir to continue the family dynasty, brought days of festival and merriment. The speed of the arrangements, both in the castle and the town, gave the impression that people had been subconsciously preparing for this day for months. Bright, colourful banners and flags hung from

doorways and upper-storey windows, bringing a sense
of carnival to the winding streets of Fenwood. Not only
did the market spring up in the square but children sold
trinkets and homemade bracelets and necklaces from
dwelling doorways, and there were numerous stalls of
freshly pressed elderflower wine and corn ale, enough to
drink for days and nights in celebration. Music could be
heard from inns and other public arenas. The Oaks set
out a seating area in the space outside the maroon front
door, where chairs and tables gave locals a chance to sit
and watch the frivolities and occasions cascade by;
Hopps (already becoming something of a Fenwood
personality) had even set up a stall to serve his Brew of
the Day for the exterior patrons. People chattered gaily
and embraced. There were smiles on faces. Fenwood
was alive. Such was the reaction and adoration that the
Queen and her King made three unceremonial visits to
the town, unaccompanied by soldiers, guardians or
advisors. The Queen courteously allowed beaming
mothers to touch her stomach, responding to their
guesses as to the baby's gender with a polite "Well, we
shall see" or "It matters not, they will be loved
anyhow". Vilius, as usual, walked two paces behind and

smiled, but could not fully hide the disdain he held for the lower classes from his miserly face. They visited the market square, where the Queen purchased several items of jewellery and lace, as well as other well-known and respected shops and establishments.

"Would m'lady like an ale?" asked Roker's son as the Queen stood at the bar of the inn surrounded by onlookers and gawkers.

"Not today, young man. Mothers-to-be are not supposed to have such drinks," smiled the royal lady, bending as she could to meet his eyes.

The boy furrowed his brow. "Is that because the baby will become drunk?"

Laughter all round.

"What is your name, young sir?" she enquired warmly.

"Haethdan, ma'am, but people here have been calling me Hopps for a long time, and I like it." A chorus of affirmation from the regulars who clinked glasses and echoed the name 'Hopps'. Spurred on by the support, he started to explain further, "You know, Hopps, like th—"

"Oh I get it. Very clever," interrupted the Queen in

jest. "Well Master Hopps, you are sure to be a fine innkeeper when your time comes, and a thousand blessings from the Gods on your taps and bottles." Roars of approval once again. "My Lord," she said, raising her voice, pretending to speak to her husband but actually addressing the room, "put coin behind the bar – these good people are thirsty for more celebration!"

*   *   *

Tolva sifted through the limited dresses that hung in the wall alcove of her chamber. She had managed to avoid the Queen due to the ceremonies and furore that had sprung up since the announcement of the royal baby-to-be. But tonight, after their final visit to the town, she had been summoned. Having declined the monarchy's invitation to accompany the Queen and her husband into Fenwood, it was perhaps inevitable. Tolva's stomach lurched as it had earlier, and as it had every time she thought of him. She had tried to bury what happened. Not spoken of it. Avoided him. Avoided the Queen. Even avoided the kindly forester who had taken her and tended to her. Yet now, as she panicked her way through her duties, she was painfully aware that, physically, she could no longer hide some of the truth.

Her knock on the royal chamber door was hesitant. As was the response. "Come."

Tolva opened the door tentatively, the droning creak only adding to the unplaceable tension. The Queen was waiting for her, centre of the room, in a high-rising cotton shirt that exposed her enlarged stomach, hands placed on the freshly oiled skin. Tolva attempted a smile but it ricocheted around her face, not hiding the awkwardness, shame and anger she felt inside. And it certainly did not take the attention away from her tunic, which now stretched around her own swollen belly. The Queen did not flinch, almost as if the moment was rehearsed or expected.

"I'd heard the rumours," she stated, unmoving, "and wanted to see if they were true." A strange, forced smile etched onto her face. "Congratulations." She paused. "You must be thrilled."

Once again, all of Tolva's plans and dreams and ideas unravelled before her; a once confident and powerful woman left a yelping shadow.

"M'lady…" she offered, "…I… I hadn't… planned on, on, on… this…"

"I know," interjected the Queen, "but it has happened."

Tolva could not read the regal lady's thoughts or feelings in her face or body. Under the black fringe, Tolva's eyes remained downcast. She wanted to say so much more, but did not have the strength to meet the royal eyes, let alone topple a dynasty with the truth.

"I had not thanked you for the part you played." By now the Queen was looking out of the window. "Thank you."

Tolva muttered something inaudible in response, but the Queen continued her outward gaze. "As a token of my gratitude, and as a means to make you comfortable, I grant you the chief guestroom as your own until… well, until you are… no longer requiring of it."

Tolva spluttered. "But that is…"

"On the other side of the castle, away from the humdrum comings and goings of castle life."

"But…"

"I cannot have you here, Tolva!" the Queen snapped, without turning. "Not…. Not…" But the words had run out.

Tolva gulped and choked on remonstrations and complaints. Inhaling purposefully, the royal mother-to-be turned to face the withering figure in the doorway.

"You are relieved of your duties. I thank you for your service."

"I…"

"You may leave now."

"But…"

"Ernest will see you out."

A heavy set, gentle-faced man had appeared behind in the corridor. His eyes were kindly, but forthright in their loyalty to his mistress, and friend. Ernest smiled.

"Come, ma'am." He held out his hand to help her, but also to let her know it was time to leave.

The Queen waited for the door to close before she allowed the air in her lungs to escape, through pursed lips at first before the restrained sobs of regret and forced necessity broke through the wall she had built up. She held her stomach as she bent over, breathing in bursts through the tears that fell. Sitting down on the bed, she steadied herself. Gliding through the darkness, the raven landed on the sill of the window. It ruffled its wings and laid its head on one side. It met the Queen's eyes as she brought her breathing back under control.

"No more," she muttered to its blackness. It squawked, spread its wings and took to the skies.

CHAPTER ELEVEN
SURVIVAL

The sound of smashing crockery brought servants running, who scattered like skittles as the King flew from the Queen's chamber in a rage. As his purple ceremonial robes disappeared around the corner, the ladies-in-waiting rushed up the stairs in fear of what might have befallen their dear monarch. They found the door open, the Queen sat on the edge of the bed but stoic in expression, with fragments of an ornate, formal plate littering the floor around her. She offered no explanation as to what had happened, barely speaking to the girls who swept the floor around her feet. Two more subservient girls wiped the scratches and ceramic dust from the wall. When they had finished, she dismissed them with a polite smile and a simple nod of her silver-haired head. The incident was never mentioned, but echoes of it ran through the corridors for some time.

News reached Tolva in her comfortable imprisonment on the far side of the castle. Despite her exclusion, the raven was by no means her only way of gathering titbits and gossip; she maintained several 'starlings' around the grounds, confidantes who flittered here and there, hearing useful news and secrets, nesting in the shadows. She was still informed but had now lost the power of influence, nullified against using the knowledge she held. She felt vulnerable, discarded, blunted. Yes, she had enjoyed the power she had garnered, revelled in it, but not for malevolent purpose. The irony that the Queen's pregnancy had given her even greater adoration from the people, whereas her own had ostracised her was not lost on Tolva. It was not an irony she could laugh at. The pain was too raw, even after all these months.

Tolva's hands massaged her aching stomach as the child within wriggled and writhed. For weeks she had struggled to gain any sense of comfort and sleeping was a rarity. Food caused her to vomit. Her ankles had started to swell up which made walking uncomfortable. But despite the discomfort, despite the rejection, despite the violence with which it had been conceived, her intuition told her that her child would be special. A force for, and from, nature. A warrior of the natural world. And no amount of degradation or fire or brutality would stop her fighting for her child. Her son. She sensed him in the movement and in her suffering. There was so much she needed him to know, to understand. The letter that she had been trying to write to him lay as a blank sheet on her desk, but now the stirring in her soul pulled her from the bed toward the desk, the quill resting easy in her hand and suddenly words flowed.

*   *   *

Hopps walked at pace, keeping alongside the sturdy frame of Kennet, the delivery man. He had begged his father to be allowed to accompany the errand run, but now as a far off howl lingered in the moonlight, he wondered whether his youthful, adventurous spirit had taken on more than he could manage. The knock on the door and night-piercing whispers had woken him, but it had been the royal crest on the man's livery that had awakened his true curiosity. What did the ruling family want with this father at that hour? It was with reluctance, and an understanding that he would be well looked after, that Hopps' father had let him go; after all, it was only a minor package, and his son had to learn sometime. But the reality was something more unsettling. The playground of winding streets by day were a cover for shadows by night. However, whilst the notion of having a guard appealed to Hopps at the outset, he was unsure if his now mute companion would really lay down his life to protect a boy laden with ale as his mind had naively imagined. Nevertheless, Hopps had promised his father to take care of the delivery and he needed to prove that he was old enough and responsible enough to deal with more tasks. A small delivery of ale to a guard nightshift seemed an ideal place to start. And as he followed Kennet through a side entrance and into meandering castle corridors, the adventure began to fulfil the spirit in which he had entered into it.

Yet it was not guards that opened the door they halted at. A thump and clatter rang out from inside before a crumpled, bearded man pulled the door toward him, a musty waft of alcohol and vomit pre-empting his dishevelled state.

"In… It opens in…" the figure muttered to either himself or the surprised visitors at the door. His tunic, which could have been nightwear or formalwear, being as it was worn without trousers or outer garments, was heavily stained.

"Have… you… Have you got… errr, what I… wanted, ordered?" When he talked his eyes lacked focus.

"Yes, sire," the guard offered before pushing Hopps forward. The boy stumbled, steadied himself, and presented the package, rattling as his hands shook.

"Are you scared of me… boy?" mumbled the man as he, also shaking, took the box.

"No," admitted Hopps, "I see men like you all the time at the inn."

The man looked visibly disgruntled.

"You see kings in your.. your inn?" the slurring man scowled. The boy, under his wavering gaze, looked confused.

"Well, no. But you're not…"

"I'm a king! Your king!" the man snapped, growling in anger. "Are you blind, boy? Look at me. LOOK AT

ME." He was shouting now, his bitterness rising to the surface through layers of ale, arrogance and forced nicety. "Am I not regal?" He puffed out his chest. "Am I not kingly?" The boy opened his mouth to say something but he had not figured out the appropriate words. "This ignorant town and its stupid people…" The man lumbered back into the room beyond, continuing his loathsome diatribe to imagined devotees. It appeared as though he was looking for something, stumbling around in the near darkness, but returned to the door, staggering and empty handed.

"I cannot find any… errr, coins, money, to give you for the, errr… the…"

"That's fine," interjected the boy, hoping to dispel the awkwardness. "Next time." He looked up at the guard, clearly expecting a sign that he could leave. The tall castle soldier nodded at the King.

"Sire." He turned, facing back down the corridor they had come.

"It was good to meet you." Hopps smiled, maintaining the pleasantry, knowing his father would expect it. "My Lord… King. And congratulations on the baby."

The response was volcanic.

"IT'S NOT MY BABY!"

Echo. An endless echo. Then silence.

"That whore... I should never... YOU CAN LISTEN TO WHATEVER RUMOURS YOU WANT BUT I NEVER..." He was frothing at the mouth. "Gods' know she could have had any number of men up in her room... You, guard, you probably... IT'S NOT MINE!" And now he was ranting to an inner darkness once again. "She comes here from nowhere, taking the Queen from me..."

Unknowingly, so innocently, Hopps' stone began the avalanche.

*   *   *

Tolva turned over, and over, and over. She could not settle. The infant within was restless, a warrior ready for battle. Her emotions turned on a pivot: panicked and desperate over lack of sleep, then calm in the knowledge that he was healthy and she needed to keep her blood flowing serenely. For him. Rolling onto her left side once again, she stuffed her bed quilt under her engorged stomach for support, laying in the dark and regulating her breathing to the soundscape of the wind and wolf calls. And so it was that she saw the parchment being slid under her door.

Her mind raced far quicker than her body could now move. It was some time before she hauled herself from the bed and crossed the cold stone floor, pulling the solid wood door open too roughly for its ageing hinges. The corridor outside was empty. With difficulty, Tolva lowered her body to an uncomfortable crouching position and, at the third attempt, picked up the paper. Instinctively, she held it to her nose and sniffed it. There was a scent of rose. She turned it over in her hands. Plain with a fine but hurried script unevenly in the centre.

'He will kill you.

Get out.'

Initially she felt no panic. Just intrigue. She instantly knew who 'he' was, but who had delivered it? And why? Again, she looked around her. A sensation. A change in the air. A stifling. A heat. Now her chest tightened.

Suddenly her eye was caught by small flickers of firelight through the turret window opposite. Fire. Guards. They were coming for her. Then she panicked.

Tolva fought for a clear thought, frantic now. She closed her eyes to shut out the distractions, the fears.

"Servant's quarters," she whispered to herself. The guards would not come via the service staircase for fear of waking the staff whose rooms they would need to pass by. Taking seconds to close her chamber door, she took to the narrow, unlit staircase obscured by decorative wall hangings, her bare feet barely making a sound. She moved swiftly in spite of her fear, teetering on the cusp of control. From above her there came a stifled ruckus, many leather shoes on flagstones, whispered orders. Tolva lost concentration on her own plight, slipped but steadied herself on the stone wall. They would discover her chamber empty at any moment. Already had. The sound of the following mob began to grow. They were on the stairs. Puffing, she stumbled and scuffed her way down.

By the time she reached the bottom, Tolva had lost her sense of how many floors she had descended, of where she was and where she was heading. The flat

ground of a corridor came up to meet her feet with a
suddenness that made her lurch forwards. She was out
of breath and sweating. Panting. Out of control. Her
hands went to her stomach. A strange sensation had
started circling. Had she banged into something? Or
disturbed the baby with her chaotic descent? Had she…
Then realisation hit her.

"No," escaped her lips on a sharp intake of breath.
From deep inside her a pain had begun to spread, an
intense pressure that grew. She had never felt anything
like it, though she knew what it meant. "No… no… not
now…" she repeated, looking down with tears welling
in her eyes. She gritted her teeth and braced herself with
a hand on the moist, cold stone wall, stifling her cries
and holding her breath. Eventually the pain passed, but
she remained hunched, supporting her body in the
darkness. Alone. Frightened. With her baby coming.

Tolva took a moment to glance around and take in
her surroundings: the dim, greenish light; the damp,
stale air of a subterranean corridor; the forgotten doors
of lesser-known storerooms. Then, realisation. She
knew this place. Moving steadily along the wall to her
left, she shifted her suffering body on shaking legs

further along the basement rows, passing wooden doors long since sealed shut by time. Every few minutes she gritted her teeth and screwed her eyes as another contraction seared through her. They were getting closer together, but at least she could hear no sound of footsteps or commotion. Then, with a rising beat in her heart, her hand touched the wood of a door she had known. The remembered trauma pushed burning bile back into her throat. She struggled to breathe. With trembling hands, the bolt opened easily, surprisingly, in her hands.

The room had been cleaned and tidied. Someone covering their tracks. The storage shelves were bare. The chair no longer oak but wicker. No stained cloths. The floor, once strewn with bloodied evidence of the chamber attack, had been polished so that the grey shine did not match the greenish hue of the corridor cobbles. As she stood looking, searching for understanding and meaning, Tolva somehow felt nothing; not numbness but a detachment. A reality that was not hers. And suddenly the pain again. Centred in her womb. Almost overwhelming. Bent double, she trapped her scream behind the bars of clenched teeth.

In her mind, she heard the howl of a wolf, the slap of a hand across her face, the clank of swords… Yet even as the contraction subsided, the distant rumble of guards did not.

All she could think of now was her boy. If something happened to her, he had to survive. Survive and challenge. And yet, confined in a musty, cramped room, she could find no options. Somewhere, but not far enough away, a clank of metal on stone reminded her of the inevitability of discovery. Beyond yearning, she thought of the kind, bearded man who had saved her, grasping at the hope that he would once again appear, hulking and secure, in the doorway. But he would… Maybe not now, but soon… If only she could get a message to him…

Frantically looking around the vacant room, it had been cleared of the boxes and materials that had cluttered the shelves before. Burlap sacks in the corner. Tolva half fell, half crawled to the corner, panicking as the metallic sounds began to echo in the corridor outside the door. She leafed furiously through the sacks looking for… something, anything. There. There between two sacks was a rogue fragment of papyrus.

Snatching it up but careful not to rip the delicate sheet, she grabbed a crumbled stone of brick from the wall. His name. She had to get his name known. Her warrior. Her flame of revolution.

A thunder of footsteps on the flagstones.

'EGAN' she scrawled in chalked stone.

*   *   *

The cool air of falling night swept her black hair from her forehead and pricked at her reddening cheeks. The trade passageway from the subterranean corridors muffled the sounds of confusion from the chasing pack. Tolva took a deep breath of the outdoors. Allowed herself a moment to close her eyes. Hands on her stomach. They won't catch us, my beautiful boy. She knew where she was headed.

By the time she left the castle grounds, the chaotic sounds of the trailing search party had dwindled and dispersed. She welcomed the murmurs of night: the soothing rush of the breeze; the distant trills and calls of animals and birds from the surrounding woodlands; occasional reverberations of life from otherwise dark and dormant houses. Fenwood lay slumbering; oblivious. Tolva stole through the empty winding streets, protected by the irregular corners and overhangs of the timber-framed buildings. Every now and again, she glanced back over her shoulder but no shadows stirred in her creeping wake. Her breath began to appear in front of her, more evident in her condition, breathing heavily and slowing as she crossed the market square.

And then she heard it. A cry that did not belong. A cry that resounded off the crooked walls.

"I KNOW YOU'RE HERE…"

She knew the voice, thick with vile rage and aged liquors.

"YOU CANNOT GET AWAY FROM ME!"

The booming vocal was disorientating, rebounding off the dense building walls. Tolva looked, with a growing sense of sickness, at the avenues that opened onto the square. Nothing.

"I WILL DESTROY YOU. AND YOUR PUP."

This time she shuffled into a laboured, floundering run.

Instinctively, the raven-haired lady made her way toward the forest. The trees would close their protective arms around her, their shielding foliage keeping her from harm. The ground under her feet turned from the trampled mud of the Fenwood streets to the stony grass bridleways that ran between the fields. She could see the line of trees rising over the immediate horizon, a saviour riding to meet her. But she still felt uneasy and turned to look back the way she had come. A figure lurched through the hedgerow-cast shadows, emerging in the moonlight, bumbling ominously in her direction, arms swaying as he lumbered on. Tolva gasped in horror. Turning her gaze back to the direction in which she was headed, she staggered on, exhaustion seizing her legs and pains continuing to spasm in her stomach. Breathing was becoming a struggle. Yet she could tell that the grotesque beast was gaining on her. She had no choice but to stumble on toward the tree line. Looming in front of her, the giant trunks looked like colossal cage bars, and suddenly she was gripped by an ominous feeling, a fateful realisation. Glancing back, the monstrous silhouette heaved onward, griping and growling and chuntering in its intoxicated fury. Tolva faced back to the dark pathways of the forest, steeling herself.

Seeing her lope along the pathway, terrified and vulnerable, the trees opened up their boughs and embraced her as a sister.

CHAPTER TWELVE
BIRTH

Tolva reached out and steadied herself against the
gnarled bark of a tree as another wave of contracted
pain coursed through her body. She grimaced audibly,
gritting her teeth, screwing up her eyes. Gradually it
passed, but she remained, panting heavily, leaning
forward. Sweat beads hung on her brow. Dragging air
into her seemingly bruised lungs, she struggled to
control her emotions. The pain would come again. She
needed to find somewhere comfortable. The swirling
night mists began to curl around her ankles, tendrils that
at first appeared threatening but helped to shift her bare
feet forwards. Tolva lumbered on, lurching from tree to
tree. Every few minutes she was struck motionless,
lightning strikes of pain, screaming into the gathering
darkness as the pain pounded on. Her fingertips clawed
at the rough tree surfaces for some kind of support, her
other hand stretched over her swollen belly. Tears of

panic, of fear, of sheer agony stung her eyes and drenched her cheeks.

"Please…" she whispered breathlessly to the night, then raised her head to the moon, watching on through the ceiling of branches. "Please, help my child…"

Tolva's collapse was cushioned by a blanket of moss at the base of an old, wizened birch. She was beyond exhaustion. The roots of the tree cradled her, supported her as she crumpled, then dragged and untangled herself to a seated position, knees up, hands planted firmly upon them. Braced. She puffed her cheeks. Her hair stuck to her forehead, plastered by sweat and mist. Her body tensed. Another one. And her scream penetrated the blackness.

"He comes… He comes. My Lords…" But the words were lost in the baying wail that issued forth and was swallowed up by the night.

*　　　*　　　*

The Queen breathed consciously in through her nose, holding firmly to a stone sill, steadying herself on the tower steps. In… Two… Three. Out… Two…

Three…

"Very good, ma'am," said the midwife, stroking the labouring mother's back as she once again took control of her breathing. She moved to take a step forward, but the elderly serving woman laid a gentle, experienced hand on the white-garbed arm.

"No rush, ma'am. Calm. Breathe." The Queen looked back with an expression of genuine warmth and squeezed her hand. "Don't you start getting emotional on me now, ma'am," she chuckled. "I'm about to pull a small human from…"

"BEA!" shrieked the regent with a hoot of laughter, before clutching her enlarged belly. "Oh… Don't make me have the baby on the stairs!"

Arm in arm, the two ladies waddled across the flagstones of the landing to the royal chamber, followed by a procession of serving girls holding in their arms towels, bowls of water and various remedies. Inside the room, more young women pressed and smoothed and tidied and wafted lavender bundles to fragrance the air. The Queen smiled politely but flinched at the claustrophobic presence. Quietly yet authoritatively, the midwife spoke.

"Ladies, you can leave the water bowls and towels on the side and leave us. And you, yes, you with the lavender, that will be enough. Margot, with me please. Just you." A number of the girls began to speak up in dissension. "Just Margot. The Queen needs calm." The girls filed out, faces etched with disappointment.

"Thank you, Bea," came a relieved voice, spoken on the exhale of a controlled contraction.

*   *   *

A pair of piercing yellow lights penetrated the night. The shattered, dark-haired figure raised its head that hung almost lifeless between its knees. Her eyes, dim and bloodshot, swimming in a haze of anguish and fire, met the oncoming shape that materialised from the depths of the forest. In front of her, the wolf stopped. It sensed the human's frailty and vulnerability. No danger. The paws barely made a sound as it padded closer, sniffing. It recognised the scent, had known it herself, many times. Looking back in the direction she had come, she barked into the night. Two more lupine shapes emerged from the undergrowth. They sloped toward their mother who nudged and mumbled in low growls until they took up positions around the fading woman, defensive and protective, looking out, on guard. Satisfied, the mother-wolf turned again to the woman, now braced against a wave of pain that pulsed through her. Facing her, the wolf gazed into the human's eyes, moving her lank hair from her forehead with a knowing move of her snout.

My strength is your strength.

The pain came again. Tolva's breath was stuck behind gritted teeth.

I will protect you. The forest will protect you.

Tolva screamed. The wolf leant into her, taking the strain of the wracking body as it hurled forward.

The child will make you stronger.

Another scream. Straining. Pushing.

You are a Mother. The Power of the Earth is within you.

*   *   *

"Breathe through it, ma'am. Brrreeeeaaaaathe…"

The midwife's oiled hands smoothed their way over the Queen's stomach as she looked intently into the eyes of the prostrate royal, who felt anything but the calm that the midwife intended to project. She wanted so much to wail her lungs and womb empty, but even in her current position, open-legged on the bed, she felt this would be considered undignified. Instead, she gritted her teeth against her latest contraction.

"Yes, ma'am, feel him wanting to enter this world…"

The Queen struggled to maintain the scream.

"Just breathe with your baby. Allow him to find his way."

Stifled groans escaped her throat and broke out through the jail of her teeth.

"In through the nose, out through the—"

"SHUT UP! JUST SHUT UP!" The words devolved into a guttural release of sound and inhibition. Sweat poured from the Queen's brow as the pain finally subsided, and she buried the tears that knew another agonising spasm was again imminent.

"King…" she managed to mutter between forced breaths. "Get him—" But she was cut off by the midwife.

"Oh I'm afraid not, ma'am, he does not need to

see… Oh…" And she, in turn, was stopped mid-sentence by the Queen's vice-like grip on her wrist. Her body had lurched forward with the force and pressure of the contraction, feeling that she could do nothing but push. Low, wolfish growling sounds escaped her as the midwife began to beam with excitement.

"I see him! Yes, ma'am, push now! He's coming!"

*　　　*　　　*

She slept. The wolf mother sniffed around her and, satisfied that the woman was breathing, took a corner of her scarf between her carnivorous teeth and pulled it over her body. At the base of the tree, the two younger wolves scuffed at the earth and kicked over debris, covering the blood and waters that had darkened the ground. The baby lay on a patch of moss in the shelter of a tree hollow where she had carefully carried him, much like she had her own. His eyes, wide, dark, unseeing, looked up at her. Tiny splayed fingers reached up at nothingness. Moving the severed, knotted cord with her nose, her rough tongue cleaned up another smudge of red-white mucus. A human child. Yet a child of the forest.

"Thank you," drifted a faint voice from behind. The wolf looked back, meeting the half-open eyes of the weak mound on the floor. The eyes fell shut once more.

My strength is your strength.

The wolf sat back on her hind legs and laid her head to rest on her front paws.

* * *

A cold, damp cloth mopped her brow. She breathed purposefully out through pursed lips. Glancing over at the midwife, the baby cradled in her arms, she felt content that all was well.

"Well, if I can say," cooed the elderly lady, starry-eyed at the babe in her arms, "not a more beautiful child have I ever seen." She stroked the child's face, before adding in an awkward tone, "Even if you are a girl." Without looking away from the babe, she called out, "Maybe it'll be a boy next time, ma'am? You know, to rule next?"

The Queen did not reply. Could not. She noted the movement of several girls at the fringes of her vision, bundling up bloodied sheets whilst others positioned themselves as sentries at the doorway. It all felt somehow distant from her, like watching a play in the Great Hall, a mirror of reality. The baby in the midwife's arms spread its fingers wide and looked around absently. That it came from her, the Queen could not reconcile. The midwife's voice broke the surrealism.

"The King suggested Carianna as a name some days ago. Shall I tell him you agree?"

The Queen, head sinking into a feathered pillow, closed her eyes.

"No," she sighed, "not a name of tradition." She searched for the voice to express the need to not stifle her daughter with expectation. "Something natural. Wild. That searches for freedom. Finds its own way."

The serving lady tickled the baby's chin.

"There's no way we can name you after some blighted weed, little one, can we, eh?" Looking up, she could see the Queen unmoving in the bed. With uncertainty, the older lady began to unbutton the nursing blouse, unsure of how to read the lack of emotion from the figure laid on the bed. "Well, there's no rush on the name, ma'am, that'll come in time.

Now," – she freed her breast from the loose shirt –

"shall I feed her…?"

CHAPTER THIRTEEN
CHAOS

The King tore through the forest, smashing bush, branch and briar. Uncontrolled. Unwavering. His purpose now savagely deteriorated into wanton destruction. He bared his teeth as he forged paths through tangled undergrowth, snarling with spittle that spat from his mouth. He knew that she had come this way. Her and the runt she was carrying. Like a man possessed, he tore at leaves and ripped the undergrowth up by the root. Animals cowered in the shadowy natural recesses, taking refuge from the destructive human force. The forest could no longer provide barrier or obstacle for the marauding beast; his blood lust now so heightened that he himself was wild.

Then, from nowhere, he was thrown from his feet by a force that crashed into his side and sent him reeling into a battalion of nettles and thorns. Outraged, he scrambled back to his feet. The broad stature of Weylin stood barring his way, axe in hand, defensive in posture, weight on his back foot. He sucked in his lips beneath his greying beard. Fear and defiance raged in his eyes.

"My Lord," he panted, "I cannot let you harm them." The King approached him, the silver of his drawn blade a contrast in a scene of greens and browns. He edged closer to the forester. "I mean it, sir. I am no fool with an axe, and I will—"

Abruptly, the air was punctured from his lungs as the cold metal sunk through his ribs into his upper chest. Vilius did not move for some moments, holding the dagger into Weylin's torso, brow furrowed, staring into his eyes, relishing the power. Then he pulled the blade out, releasing a crimson river and maintaining his stance as the large man slumped first to one knee before crumpling to his side, staining the leaves with blood. The King looked down and, wordlessly, bent to the dying man and again, plunged the knife through his flesh, this time at the base of the neck, snapping the collar bone and unleashing another oozing torrent of deep red onto the earth below. A third blow entered the upper back and by the time the fourth came, clumsily penetrating the shoulder, Weylin's life was draining from his body.

Holding the blade up, the King watched a droplet of blood run down the cold metal and obscure his reflection. He did not give the body on the floor a second glance as his attention was turned again to the direction of his travel. Despite the hold up, she could not have gone far. Setting off, this time he tried to keep his movements sleek, placing his feet to incur less sound, now predatory rather than vengeful. With darkness settling in, Vilius was forced to rely on other senses than just his sight. Whilst his eyes slowly adjusted to the gloom he could make out the rudimentary leaf-strewn path by the glimmering moonlight. Around him, the forest was alive with vengeful sounds: creaks, groans, cracking and snapping, growls, cries... an infant's cry... He stopped. Tensed. There it was again. Off to his left. Trying to control his adrenaline, Vilius hastily picked his way through the trees. He knew that he needed to quieten his footsteps on the natural debris but the desperation he felt drove him onward. Blood pulsed strongly through him, his heartbeat a rising crescendo in his ears, punctuated by the occasional infant squawk from somewhere ahead. He could contain his voice no longer.

"I know you're there. You cannot escape me." Eyes penetrating the darkness, he pointed the stained dagger and slashed at the humid air. "COME FACE ME!" The bestial flash flickered in his eyes. "I can smell your fear. You and your pup." He exaggerated sniffing the air. "Frightened pup. And the bitch." His leering smile twitched. "Come on out. Bitch," he repeated with menace.

It was her eyes that pierced the night first. Vilius saw them desperate, vulnerable yet fierce. As she materialised from the darkness, her black hair hung damp from the mist, crawling on hands and knees from the undergrowth. He almost cackled.

"There she is, the b—" He was startled into obedient silence by a savage banshee screech that leapt from her rasping throat. He recoiled at this unforeseen power, that of a wounded animal, the ferocity of a mother protecting her child. Vilius thrust the knife forward once more, now in defence rather than a predatory action.

"You do not frighten me," she snarled. "I may well be terrified for my child, but I will never cower before so insidious a man." She spat as she spoke, hurling the words at him.

"You… You… enchantress!" he yelled stutteringly. This time it was her who laughed. "You.. You bewitched me. That child, that boy, is not mine…"

"No," she interjected, "he is nothing of yours. He belongs to me. He belongs to the forest. He belongs to the wild."

Tolva was closer now and began to raise herself to her feet. He kept the blade steady. She stood, a shield of defiance, inches from the pointed tip, unmoving, unwavering. Their eyes met. The once-great man, often so empowered by his title and masculinity, saw before him the incarnation of the world around him; the ferocity of a wolf, the freedom of a bird, the bringer of life. But more than this, he saw acceptance of chaos, of sacrifice, of death. Then, in a low voice deep in her chest, from another world, the dark-haired woman summoned forth incantations, indistinguishable words. Vilius flinched, his discomfort palpable, but this only made her strength grow.

"Stop that." He flinched anxiously. The intensity of her unbroken gaze haunted him. "I said stop it," he appealed again. This time she took a step forward, a show of power designed to break him. Instinctively, he lashed out and the bloodied blade tore open the flesh of her cheek. Tolva's lips curled back and teeth flashed, gritted together. Deep from her soul came a growling sound that reverberated on the boughs around her; *Keep back*, it warned, *for I am the embodiment of protection and instinct and ferocity. And I will kill you, for love.* Threatened, weakened, demoralised, Vilius could think of nothing else but to strike out in fear. A glancing blow that split her lip. Blood mixed with saliva, running down her chin. Impulsively, she reached to grab the knife, but was returned with force upon her forearm; a deep gash opened up, wounding her. He sensed her vulnerability and sliced down again, the sharp edge tearing her shoulder. Tolva fell to one knee, steadied herself, and as the King sought a fatal blow, her now blood-soaked hand snatched his wrist.

My strength is your strength.

With renewed force, he pushed the dagger down toward her heaving chest.

My strength is your strength.

The sharp metallic tip broke the skin, drew blood.

My strength…

Suddenly the pain in his leg was like his entire calf muscle had been ripped away. Losing all thought of self-centred vengeance, he looked back, and indeed it had. Staring wildly at him, the ferocious eyes of the she-wolf glowed yellow as crimson stained the grey fur beneath her fangs, a chunk of his leg hanging in tattered shreds from her jaws. Only then, in staggered realisation, did he scream. The wolf mother tossed the human flesh unceremoniously to the side, where two salivating wolves lay in wait. But this was her battle. She snarled, growled, lowered her head to pounce on her prey. Vilius' attempt to turn was laboured, agonising and pitiful. She waited for the opportune moment and sprung at the arm that held the weapon. It flew from his grasp the instant her sharp teeth sunk into his right forearm, ripping and mauling. Whilst the hand remained attached, the muscle and tissue and sinews were ravaged. The scream that threatened to hurl forth was rendered silent in utter panic and torturous pain. The wolf sat back on her haunches, her blood-stained face a picture of nature's violent, brutal power. His face turned back to her, mouthing words that no sound reached.

Again, she leapt. Her jaws closed around his throat, unrelenting and unremitting. The King struggled, contorted, gripping on to any semblance of life but unable to wrestle the wolf from him. Finally, with a twist of her head, Vilius' throat was wrenched away from his neck in an explosion of blood and fibrous tissue, and a shattering crack of his upper spine. The King's mangled body thudded to the floor, unrecognisable in its destruction. Calmly, the wolf mother sniffed once, twice, before placing a paw upon her victim in a symbol of victory and justice.

*   *   *

Tolva shivered. The cold seeped in through her open wounds, ghosted along her veins and penetrated her heart. Her face was wet with blood, the taste of iron strong in her mouth. She could see the wolf pawing at the King's body, chewing at the ripped flesh. She tried to raise her right arm but the tendons in her shoulder had been shredded. Struggling to move her neck, she could see down to where her arm was now only partly attached to the collar. And there was a lot of blood. So much blood. Too much. Tolva retched at the sight, bile stinging her throat and falling down her cheek to the ground. A younger male wolf sidled alongside her prostrate frame, steam rising from its fur in the descending night air, but a low growl from its mother called it away. Stretching out her left hand, Tolva grasped into the dampening ground and hauled her body forward. She felt numbness, no pain. No hope. All she could think of was her boy.

"E…" was all she could manage in a breathless whisper. Another ungainly drag along the forest floor. And another, her fingernails splintering on the dried, fallen foliage. Suddenly her hand hit something different. Soft to touch, and yet solid, like moss on a rock. Adjusting to the gloom, her eyes could make out a black shape, small, twisted, with onyx circles that glinted in the moonlight. A beak. Wings. It was then that Tolva knew.

Her mouth still coated in the remains of her feast, the wolf sniffed at the limp female body before her. She had found the black-haired lady once before, desperate and vulnerable, but not without fight, not like this. Crimson stained the clothing, stuck with twigs and leaves. Laying her head on the figure's back she could feel the faintest rise and fall. But there would not be many more. The wolf mother lay down next to Tolva, her warmth trickling across to the stricken woman. They lay together for some time; the night waiting patiently, the forest silent in respect. A cloud moved in front of the moon. The wolf sniffed, licked Tolva's face, groaned. Her rough tongue moved lank strands of black hair from the deathly pale face.

She opened her mouth to speak. The wolf's ears pricked up and she raised her piercing eyes. "…Child… Egan…"

Their eyes met. Held. Then the light finally faded in the woman and the look became an unseeing stare. Watching her essence float away, the wolf mother barked her farewell:

I will protect him. The forest will protect him.

CHAPTER FOURTEEN

CELEBRATION OF LIFE

A blood moon ruled over the forest. The wild mists and the tumultuous storm subdued their threats and drifted away on the valley winds. The reddish hue of the night sky glowed like fire over the luminous moon, standing high and proud.

The shades of death hung stiflingly over the woodland. The aftermath of the night's savagery lay in a swathe of flesh and blood over the forest floor. Taking advantage, a young male wolf picked, slathering, at the remains of a carcass, cleaning the ribs before sniffing the ground for a fresh kill. Sliding between the tall blades of grass, he encountered another body, complete but stained crimson, bearing the marks of violent struggle. He padded closer; the scent was different. Something recognisable. A guttural groan rumbled in the wolf's throat as he trapesed his nose over the body, the neck, the face, licking at the clotted blood that was forming at the gashes in the skin. He knew the man. The forest man. Sniff. Alive. He took a few soft steps back and looked at the human's size; too big and heavy to move by himself. Stretching his neck, he raised his head to the red glowing moon and howled, low and long, signalling for help from his brother. The sound echoed through the trunks and tracks, searching out his lupine family. Waiting patiently, he lay next to the stricken body, his warmth slowly passing to the near-lifeless man.

*   *   *

A muted lull hung in a suffocating mist over the castle as the sanguine moon waned and relinquished the night to a reluctant sunrise. The birds sensed the closeness and kept to their nests; no birdsong heralded the morn. Light crept in like a thief at the corners of rooms, drawing long shadows across cold floors. The cry of the cockerel stuttered and was lost into a whimper. There was an unknown, an uncertainty, an ominous disquiet.

Work began late and remained sluggish and forced throughout the day. Light-hearted chatter was tucked into pockets and the often-heard singing never left the tool stores. Frequently, eyes looked out from under the brims of hats and strayed in the direction of the castle, shrouded in an eerie silence. No flag flew. No heralds cried. No buzz of activity. Lifeless. Dormant.

Inside the perimeter walls, the castle appeared deserted. Crates and boxes from the previous day's deliveries stood in toppling stacks in corners. Horses hung their heads, coated, steam drifting from their nostrils in the fresh morning air. Two rats darted here and there, nibbling at abandoned food scraps. A young boy stepped out from the cold recess of an archway into the cobbled courtyard, scattering the bickering rodents; the sound of the twigs in his brush scraping on the stone echoed against the walls, an irritant in an awkward sideshow. He slowed to a stop, the stifling silence oppressive, and slunk away.

The corridors of the castle building were hauntingly quiet, punctuated only by the soft shuffle of light footsteps or the distant clanging of pots from the basement that echoed up the empty passageways.

Servants walked in the shadows, their nervous footfalls swallowed up by the nothingness of the walled walkways. The Master of Ceremonies paced the floor of his private office, anxious about arrangements for upcoming festivals and services, but very much aware of the mood of the town. Mrs Maltcross held back on the number of dishes she served at formal dinner times, and yet still received untouched plates and platters when the depleted number of sitters had left the table. Messages were left unsent. Orders left unfulfilled. Appointments missed. A nervousness hung over Fenwood. There had been a change in the breath of the wild. Now the town collectively, restlessly, waited.

*   *   *

Weylin's eyes flickered and gradually stuttered open. His first breaths were gasps, filling his lungs with close, humid air. Then the torment in his neck, shoulders and abdomen rushed up to meet him. He grimaced, teeth clenched, straining against the scream that strived to escape. With the pain throbbing, he glanced down. A peculiar large, flat leaf covered his upper chest and shoulder on his right side. Reaching over and lifting it, both wounds underneath appeared raw and ominous, but clean and had been crudely filled with a paste made from leaves and herbs, such was the smell that arose. The realisation that he had been tended to struck him and he looked around for the person who had saved him. He was clearly inside, somewhere, and as his eyes adjusted to the dimness, he could make out branches and compacted mud in the surrounding walls. A groan escaped Weylin's mouth as a sharp, searing agony ripped through his back and shoulders, more than clenched teeth could withstand. Involuntary tears pricked his eyes and he laid his head back, waiting for the stabbing sensation to pass. Finally, as it subsided, he was able to lift his head and looked down beyond his feet. A hazy light glowed in an opening, the sun itself tentatively watching down from her position above the trees. There, silhouetted in the doorway, stood a wolf.

*   *   *

The Queen looked down at the babe mewling and gargling in her arms. The little fingers flexed and relaxed, unblinking dark eyes looking but not seeing. Placing her index finger next to the curling baby digits, she did not grip. Across the room, Ernest lined up skirts and dresses on a rail, putting together a selection for the River Music festival that evening, as his mistress liked to have the last choice herself. He glanced and smiled at the mother and daughter perched on the edge of the lounging chair, like a painting of a nurturing goddess. Without looking up, her voice drifted to him as if she spoke from a dream.

"I'm not going tonight, Ernest. I want to be here." Ernest did not outwardly show any emotion, any judgement.

"Ma'am, the people want to see you."

"Yes," she replied, annoyed but maintaining her calm manner, "but they will understand that I now have a child, and my place is here, with her."

"Indeed, ma'am." But he had not finished. "Yet it is that very little one that means they demand your attention, your company, just a sight of you, even more." He turned to face her, emboldened. "And if I may say, ma'am, they do not see you as just her mother. You are their Mother, now." She looked up at her serving master, expecting him to look away, but he held her gaze and even raised his eyebrows in a gesture of hopeful agreement. A smile hinted at the corners of her eyes.

"Will you look after her, then, Ernest? Clean her when she…"

"Oh, m'lady, you have far more qualified ladies for that!" He turned back to the silks and satins, the cottons and collars. The Queen could see that his shuffling and folding and re-hanging was unnecessary, repetitive, as though he wanted to say more. Every now and then he glanced up; she pretended to be wrapped up in the baby, whose eyes were blinking themselves shut. Then suddenly, he spoke.

"You can't hide her here." The comment touched a nerve. The Queen said nothing but silently fretted over thoughts that she had long refused to confront. Ernest, not looking round, had not read the signs. "Because the people are clamouring to see their princess…"

"She's not *their* princess," came the snapped retort. "She's *my* daughter."

Ernest turned and looked at his Queen, pained that he had upset her but equally determined that someone

162

needed to give her this truth. "Of course she is your daughter… but in some ways she also belongs to them, just as you do… or at least a version of you…" She knew he was right, and even though she opened her mouth to say something, no sound came out. "Of course, it's completely up to you," he continued, backing himself out of the difficult position he had put himself into. "The people will love you no matter what, and you have always—"

"Yes." The interruption was short through forced acceptance rather than annoyance.

"Sorry, ma'am?"

"I said, yes."

"I know, ma'am, but yes to w—"

"Yes. Yes, I'll take her out. To meet people."

Ernest nodded serenely, with no expression, just duty.

"Very good, ma'am."

"But not today." Her words were staccato, pushed out through understood need rather than motherly protection. Ernest nodded again in dutiful understanding.

"I believe that the children's crafts celebration will be

upon us in several days. We could arrange for it to be held in the castle grounds this year. For your comfort."

The Queen exhaled, a faint smile nervously touching the corners of her mouth.

"Yes, that sounds agreeable. Thank you, Ernest."

This time a shallow bow, no nod.

"Not a problem, ma'am. I shall speak with the Master of Ceremonies as soon as can be."

*   *   *

The castle grounds were turned into a playground for the event, which elevated the fayre far beyond previous years. Tents were erected to house various different craft workshops, from cloth dying to ring making. There were entertainers dotted around, sparking spontaneous crowds to assemble at their latest card disappearing trick or feat of balancing or juggling. Faces were painted and songs were sung. The Queen walked gingerly round, her smile never fading or failing. She talked openly behind her regal front to the folk who clamoured for just a few seconds of her attention. She smiled at the right moments. She sympathised with their plights and woes. She knelt to talk to the children. Then, when the time came for her to take her turn with the entertainments, she allowed herself to be foolish and be laughed at. But her eyes showed signs of discomfort, a vacant look, a detachment from the people. Her people.

"Ma'am, I think it's time."

The outpouring of adulation was euphoric. The appearance of the royal princess at the festival released the tides of gifts, well-wishes, flowers at the castle doors. Those present at the children's craft celebration were pressed by family and friends for every minute detail of the baby girl, and were able to hold avid listeners in a mesmerised stupor as they relayed the events of that afternoon in the castle grounds. In Fenwood, what followed were weeks, months of ceremonies and celebrations. A public party in the market square. A private naming ceremony before the public announcement of the name:

Ivy.

Natural, beautiful, but wild.

Those with the responsibilities of upholding Fenwood's formal traditions were kept busy, engaged in completing documents, finding correct robes, rehearsing forgotten lines of scripture. The castle was once again alive with people and gifts and food. Shops and businesses in the town flourished with the need to feed and entertain party guests of all ages, and to dress them in new outfits for each occasion. In the midst of it all the Queen relished her longed-for role, devoting herself to her daughter. She proudly carried the beautiful babe-in-arms to public gatherings, holding for all to see, allowing townsfolk to stroke and kiss and bless Ivy, the most yearned for of children. When the need arose, the Queen was not afraid to embrace the natural needs of motherhood, openly feeding the baby in public, and whilst some found this uncomfortable and unnecessary, it gave rise to the whispered nickname 'Mother' that then took wings and flew, cementing her iconic status and granting her an enduring name to bear into legend.

* * *

The wolf licked the droplets of fallen milk from the boy-child's face. He lay swaddled in a cloth and furs, sheltered behind a rocky outcrop in the dense forest, almost impenetrable to human kind. Padding forward onto a stone shelf, she subtly sniffed the air, eyes piercing the wood mist, expecting the return of her hunting offspring. Not detecting their scent, she let out a low, searching howl. No answering call came back. They must be far abroad. Behind, the human infant whimpered, an unsettled mewling of growing distress, so, returning, the wolf mother laid down next to him, shielding his body from the breeze. His fumbling fingers found the dense fur of her upper chest, soothing himself with the touch. Lowering her head, she nuzzled him comfortingly. As she listened to his gurgling breaths she knew she would have to make the journey soon. Having watched the Man, she could sense his compassion and affinity with nature. She had lain in the bush-cover, observing his movements: his calm, safe demeanour with the animals of the forest; his thoughtful understanding in his treatment of the trees; his sturdy and polite distance from his fellow humans… as though he were of the forest, not of the human world. She knew not whether he could raise a child but she trusted that his intentions would be true.

*   *   *

Weylin's leather boots trudged the muddied pathway, deep into the forest, away from Fenwood life. The rope taut around his waist dragged a small cart on log wheels laden with firewood, gathered from fallen trunks and boughs. Despite his laboured gait, he did not falter in his journey at fork or obstacle. Whilst he had a homestead, a shelter under the trees, the forest was his home; he knew it, loved it, understood it, like a brother or sister, or Mother. It had saved him, provided for him, and now he worked daily for its survival and prosperity.

Pushing aside groping shrubbery with his worldly hands, Weylin entered the relative clearing where the hof sat camouflaged by the background of tall trees and wooden foliage. The lumbering man tried to keep his eyes ahead of him, but the spiritual house held such affinity for him that his eyes strayed in its direction from under unkempt eyebrows. As he did so, a movement in the doorway drew his attention and he slowed his pace, untying the knotted rope around his midriff and bringing the trailer to a halt. The door to the hof swung gently in the breeze, no longer secure after the violence of the raider attack. Weylin was careful as he opened it inwards, not wanting to break it from its hinges or disturb whatever was inside. Glancing down at the threshold, he sighed at the memory of crimson blood and the severed, ravaged hand.

His eyes did not need to adjust to the dark. She was lying with her back to the far wall, head resting on her front paws. A dull light glowed in her eyes, but submissive, receptive. As the man entered she raised her head, baring no teeth but engaging with his presence with her alertness. He paused as he caught sight of her, but reading no threat in her movements, he took several tentative steps forward.

"Didn't think I would find you here, girl?" he ventured. Her lupine eyes followed him in the dim light. "Have you been living here?" The wolf opened her mouth and allowed a strangled rumble to escape. It did not catch his attention, so she tried a deeper growl. This time the tall human looked back at her and she inclined her head toward the fireplace. On first glance he could see some cloth. "What have you got there?" He moved closer. "Does one of your cubs need help?"

The wolf stood as he bent to his haunches, reaching out his hands to the bundle behind the grille. His gasp was audible. With surprising gentleness, he lifted the fabric-wrapped load from its protective shield in the small hearth. Peeling back folds, a face was revealed. A human face. The baby seemed even smaller in Weylin's large hands. Incredibly, the child, sleeping soundly, was clean, healthy and safe. Weylin beheld the wolf with awe, her yellow, imploring eyes flicking between the face of the towering man and the precious child in his arms.

"You have... nourished this babe?" Somehow he knew the answer. "Extraordinary." He knelt in sheer admiration and wonder. "Wolf mother." She allowed him to run his wizened hands through her ragged grey fur; she closed her eyes at his touch, confident she had made the right choice. The man, however, faltered. "Now, you think... I cannot..." The wolf had already bowed her head and begun plodding toward the door. Again, the man stammered, "I am not a mother..." But the wolf was nosing the door ajar and did not look back.

*　　　*　　　*

The boy fitted into a crate that the forester had found in an outbuilding, lining it with burlap and straw stuffing. He sat staring at the baby who wriggled calmly in his makeshift crib. Weylin had mentally run through various people, families, wet-nurses, anyone who could raise the boy, who could provide him with everything he needed to survive, to learn from, to prosper. A thought planted itself in his mind and grew: here was the child of the forest, birthed into wilderness, sustained by the wild. And nobody understood that better than him. He placed his large, stained hand comfortingly on to the baby's chest; instinctively his tiny fingers grasped a grubby digit and squeezed.

"What do you think, boy? Are you ready for a life in the wild?"

CHAPTER FIFTEEN
AFTER

The Great Crossroads were alive with the wooden trundling of laden carts. Weather-beaten faces smiled as the kindly signpost informed them that their journey to Fenwood was nearly fulfilled. The tones and accents of many travelled voices blended harmoniously in a patter of camaraderie:

'How far have you come?'

'It is long since last I saw you, my friend!'

'Where are you purchasing your silks these days?'

'Is it true, the Queen has a child?'

'You must visit the hof – no city has one so steeped in tradition…'

'Have you got your stall reserved?'

'My friend, you must try…'

Parading over the crest of the hill, the tradesfolk braced the weight of their trucks into their arms and shoulders and descended the slope into Fenwood, and market day.

The market square was alive with triumphant sounds and cries, intoxicating smells and spellbinding colours. Abundant stalls and carts lined the walkways, the calls of the sellers enticing unwitting buyers, sirens in the cacophonic buzz of the festival. Here, day-long roasted ham was pulled from the bone and loaded into freshly baked bread rolls, smothered in butter freshly churned from local cattle, salivating at the building of such bountiful provender. There, hand-sculpted rings of mountain-river silver slid onto the dainty fingers of maidens who turned in wide-eyed pleas to the trapped man at their side. Market day was a bountiful array of brewed drinks, fresh produce, medicines in vials, tobacco, spices, silks and so much more, all funnelled into Fenwood along the Great Crossroads from the wide world that lay as mysteries beyond its borders.

The Queen smiled warm greetings and tipped her head at the many addressings of 'my Queen', 'M'lady' and even 'Mother' as she meandered her way through the corridors of stalls. The crowds parted as she moved, her silvery-white gown a contrast to the hues of greens and browns that blended to her sides. Clutching her hand, a small child tottered unsteadily next to her, both overwhelmed and oblivious to the furore around them. The little girl, now approaching her fourth year, was growing used to crowds of people and gawping eyes. Every so often she pulled her mother to a stall that drew her attention with colour or wonderous objects, but nothing took her fancy more than the soft bird toy that she carried against her chest. They walked with no guard or entourage, feeling safer amongst the people than anywhere (although castle marshals, dressed in townsfolk clothing, positioned themselves at various sight-line points around the market square). Events of years past had begun to fade from memory, existing now only as nightmares comforted by the soft breathing of the little girl, Ivy, sleeping next to her.

The passing of the King had been announced without cause. The people of Fenwood had assumed ill health, probably due to his much-whispered love of wine and mead and apple-beer. There had been a traditional 'Ceremony of Passing' but no public funeral, and whilst the Queen had observed a period of mourning, this had not been declared for the people. In time his name was lost from the history of Fenwood, further cementing the legend of the Mother, the indomitable female. In turn, Ivy's narrative was fatherless, a child of immaculate conception; no person knowing how truthful, ultimately, that myth was. Fenwood itself became iconic and travellers would arrive drawn by the symbol of royalty, of female power, and its symbiosis with the land. It was some way across the land before the Peasant's Way connected Fenwood to the next city, and so it avoided influence and development. It remained an island in the mists of time, clinging to its traditions and ceremonies and unwavering trust in the old ways.

As a young girl, Ivy enjoyed everything that came with being the daughter of the Queen. Life was a succession of chances to wear new clothes, eat a variety of foods and meet interesting people. The castle was her playground, an endless source of adventure and exploration. When she fell, someone picked her up. When she was lonely, someone entertained her. When she erred, a protective and comforting hand guided her. Often she was taken out and led around the fields, the stores, the dwellings; the Queen and castle staff were keen for the young princess to understand and appreciate not only her privilege in life, but also the important and vital roles that the people of Fenwood fulfilled. However, she was young and that lesson would take time to instil. When market day came around it was difficult to teach Ivy the bigger picture of value and worth when there were so many colourful and pretty trinkets to hold and finger and demand.

Ivy rolled a figurine in her tiny, clumsy fingers, standing at a toy stall. She had slid her hand from her mother's who had stopped to politely talk to a local farmer about his sausage making technique, making her way through a thin crowd to a stall that had caught her eye.

"Mummy. Mummy?" Her curly hair flicked round as she searched around her, but looked only into the midriffs of her collection of minders. "Where is Mama?" she crowed, at which several of the staff shushed her in unison.

"She'll be here soon." A usual reply. Ivy harrumphed and put the figure of a shepherdess down grumpily, where it toppled. With furrowed eyebrows the small girl stomped dramatically towards the end of the market thoroughfare. As she reached the entrance to the lane between the fields, two castle servants caught up with her little trotting legs.

"Where are you going, miss?" came a voice with forced kindness through breathless fatigue. The child kept up her rehearsed frown and strutted onward.

"Miss?" a second servant enquired. Without turning, the girl grumped.

"I want to see the woods. I have never been." Despite the remonstrations of the following pack, Ivy marched on down the stony, grassed path between the hedgerows until the stately columns of oak and birch towered up in front. Then her feigned confidence and youthful ignorance failed her. Awe struck her. The magnificence.

"It's alright, my wild one." A familiar soothing voice and comforting hand on her shoulder. She shrunk into her mother's skirts. "Baby, there is nothing to fear. The forest is old, yes, and powerful, but there is nothing to fear." The Queen crouched to speak softly into her daughter's ear. "You, of all people, have nothing to fear." Standing again, she held out an ageing hand, indicating for her daughter to take it. "Come."

*   *   *

"Mummy, my legs hurt." The little girl's shoulders had dropped along with the corners of her mouth. Feet planted, refusing to move. "Mummy!" The Queen could not hear her.

Ahead, the Great Crossroads flickered with light through the natural canopy above, the breeze shifting the leaves and a kaleidoscope of colours shimmered the surrounding bushes and trunks. Continuing her slow pace forward, the Queen listened to the voices on the wind. Some spoke of the town of Fenwood, some of a slumbering power deep in the heart of the forest. Others sang a mournful song of sorrow for the loss of the green witch. For the first time in the passing of many seasons, she thought of Tolva. Never had she been more afraid of someone who she knew she could trust implicitly. A woman with such power and fragility. Chaos and peace.

"Mummy!" As the older lady turned to look at her daughter, a change came over the expression of the princess. "Are you sad, Mumma?"

"No, baby." The Queen pushed a smile to the

forefront. "I'm just remembering a special lady." The little girl put her head to one side, trying to understand more from her mother's vulnerable face. "Without her, I wouldn't have you."

"Why?" It was definitely a question the Queen was not ready to answer.

"Because… Because she helped me find you in the forest."

The little girl considered the answer. "Was she a sorceress?"

The Queen smiled. "No. But she was magical. In many ways."

Ivy pouted as she thought hard. "Mummy, did she have any children?"

CHAPTER SIXTEEN

EGAN

Overhead, trouble was brewing. Grey grappled with white, wrenching control of the skies to its meddlesome ways. Silhouetted birds panicked, fleeing the ensuing boisterous brawl in droves, searching for calm away from the gathering turmoil. The wind swayed and swirled, changing direction and whispering the wrath of the Gods. Morning was waning as the forest prepared itself for turbulence; for change.

The door of the small, hand-constructed dwelling burst open and a stooping figure bounded out across the glade and into the cover of the treeline. It barely rose from its crouched position, using its front limbs to propel its body forward, somewhat beast-like in movement, feral in demeanour. Moments later, a burly, grey-haired man appeared in the doorway, stepped out into the misty air, looked furtively around at the surrounding trees. He exhaled in mental exhaustion.

"Lorcan? LORCAN! Lorc…" He could not even bring himself to finish. Inside, Weylin knew that the boy could never be tamed. He had been born into chaos, succoured by beasts and protected by the forest; the wild flowed through his blood. Weylin had spent time instructing the youngling but it was a futile act, not only to go against the nature of the creature but also to pretend that he, Weylin, was anything different from a refined brute himself. Now, as the boy grew independence and will, despite his infant age, it had become impossible to control him; to cage him.

The swinging door flung back against the huge, hulking frame of the man who gingerly held his body, occasional spasms of pain in his shoulders and upper body. His physical wounds had healed, but he was left once again with a stark reminder of why he had all but disappeared from public view. Picking up a clay pot filled to the brim with a milky liquid, his hand shook. Weylin's strength had depleted through injury and age, and he knew that he could do no more for the boy. Reaching back to the door, he closed the bolt across and turned his back on the world.

*   *   *

The trodden grass path disappeared quickly beneath the pounding feet and hands of the boy-beast, gliding effortlessly through brush and briar, pausing here and there to sniff the air and taste the breeze. His limbs burned with the effort of running and the thrill of freedom. His ears pricked at the distant murmur of water, a brook somewhere to his left. He allowed his senses to guide him to its edge, the soft banking verge cooling his feet. Cupping his hands, he dipped them into the frolicking water and brought them, trickling, to his mouth. The refreshment was not enough. Stooping, he plunged his lower face into the waters, lapping with his tongue until sated. Wiping away the droplets that ran down his chin, the wild-child checked his location with tilts and flicks of his forest-streaked head. That way. He took to his haunches and powered on.

At the fringes of the forest, he slowed to a careful pace of stealth. Picking his way, using the hedging as a shield, the creature hugged the border of the forest, watching the people in their ways that he could not comprehend. The marks and smudges of his woodland habitat hid him from plain sight, a camouflaged observer of the orchestrated order of urban life. Here and there, people moved back and forth: some quickly whilst others walked slowly; some carrying sacks or objects which the boy pondered over their purpose; some looking around them and issuing forth greetings as others kept their heads down in private consultation. None noticed the figure on the fringes of the wild.

With renewed purpose, his claw-like hands pushed aside the leafed foliage and continued stealthily along the coverage towards the white castle. Of late he had felt an urge to enter within the walls, with his childish and impetuous mind not considering the dangers or even a reason why. On days where he had run off from the shack in the woods, he had squeezed his body, still plump in its boyishness, through gaps and archways until he had stood inside its boundaries. On the last journey he had discovered a stairway in the ground that led into the building itself. Then he had stalled, afraid of what was inside. But today he had resolved to enter.

Contorting himself through an arched window, the forest child dropped noiselessly to his haunches on the gravelled mud ground. Looking furtively around, he could neither see, hear or sense human activity. Satisfied as to his safety, he crossed the grounds on hands and feet, hurrying into the relative cover of the castle wall. Traversing the rough stone at his back, he clambered over jutting, solid foundations until he could see the steps in the ground, a subterranean entrance. Pausing momentarily at the top to sniff the air warily, his feet descended the damp, downward flight.

The corridor below was stale and musty, the smell of things lost and long forgotten. The moss growing on the walls was pleasant, comforting to his touch, but a sign that people did not come here. To both the left and right, the dingy passageways curved slightly until out of sight, endless bare, grime-smudged walls broken up by occasional wooden doors, untold and disregarded secrets beyond.

His attention was drawn by something to his right side; a vague feeling, an inner voice. Moving cautiously, hands picking his way before his feet, aware suddenly that the slightest sound reverberated off the damp inner-castle rock. Pausing here and there to inspect a crater or rut, or to sniff the ground, the creature made his way in the direction he was being inextricably drawn.

Meaningless wooden entrances passed by. Then, like an ominous shadow lurching from the darkness, he felt his chest tightening as he rounded a meandering curve. His infant legs and chubby fingers slowed their pace. Further on ahead was a door that looked like every other. But his stomach turned. His lungs constricted. As he approached, stooping until he crawled like a vigilant beast, the scent in the air was distantly familiar. A vague something... someone...

Almost surprisingly, the handle of the time-worn door turned easily, rolling with a click before giving in with a slight barge of the shoulder which unstuck the years of concealment. The room within was empty, but as the door edged open the child was hit by a rush of voices, emotions, revelations. Clouded visions of blood and pain and wolfish snarls, nausea and chaos. He reeled back, screwing his eyes. His head swam with nightmares of torn flesh, bawling newborns, clamouring armies, accompanied by a thudding beat that may have been the panicked beating of his own heart. As the barrage subsided, he blinked several times. The room had changed, an otherworldliness, as if seeing it through other eyes. Papers, boxes, pot-lined shelves stacked against the walls. Floor littered with sacks, cloth. And blood. An empty chair. The aura of a figure. In distress. The boy could feel their panic, could feel their determination. Chaotic focus. A focus that… His eyes were dragged toward the wall, fixating on the crumbling corner of a slab. His heart pounded, tightened, both desiring and suppressing the urge to uncover the fateful energy within. Carefully, cautiously, his trembling fingers faltered at the chalking stone. Against all expectancy the corner of the stone came away in his calloused hand. Letting it drop to the floor as crumbled debris, his teeth clenched at the scrap of rolled paper revealed in the small cavity beyond. With surprising tenderness, his fingers pulled the paper from its temporary retreat. It was browning, frail with time, crisp to touch. But it unrolled with ease. Plain, except for one word scrawled in the middle. Hurriedly, he wracked his brain for the lessons Weylin had tried to teach him.

E

G

A

N

E – G – A – N

Egan.

Egan.

Egan.

It was a word. Just a word. But he knew, somehow. From somewhere deep within his very being, he knew. It was his past. His family. His identity. The ground on which he walked. His existence. He became aware that his heart was drumming. Or it had stopped beating. He couldn't be sure.

Egan.

Egan.

Questions swam in gathering tears in the deep pools of his eyes. The realisation of the figure who had fought, battled, for him. A mother. His mother. So that he could live. So that he could have a name. His name.

From far away he heard a voice drifting through the underground tunnelled corridors; fragments of whispers that penetrated his utopian imaginings.

"…saw it from a window… down the trade steps… must have come this way…"

The broken words dragged him back to his

surroundings: the musty room, the damp walls, the precious paper in his trembling hands. There was so much that he did not understand, that he wanted to sniff out and explore. His eyes, usually so alert and aware, stung with the need to cry. His chest heaved with breaths that came in deep waves, overwhelming and unfathomable. The surge of emotions was too intense; he needed time, but he could not risk discovery. With one final glance down, he whispered the word to himself once more, his eyes closed, knowing it to be his.

"Egan."

The boy, standing now erect, pressed his wiry body to the cracking door frame. Muted footsteps could be heard on the flagstones, but the subterranean ricochet made it difficult to determine the direction of the sound. Tilting his head, he waited again for the murmur of intrusion. Waited. Waited. There. The sharp rap of wood on stone. His head flicked upright, furtively hypervigilant. No time. Go.

The flat face of a metal spearhead collided with his nose. Disorientated by raw emotion and resounding echoes, his senses had been blunted. He had darted from the storeroom, immediately heading back in the direction he had come. A noise behind had startled him and, turning, the metal crashed down on his fragile, vulnerable face. His little body hit the cold floor, whimpering and shaking at the shock of the blow. Around him, the castle guards gathered, guiltily looking down at the wretch, fidgeting and whining.

"Is it… human?" one asked from beneath an untrimmed, thick moustache. He lowered the butt of his pike to its protruding ribs, expecting the creature to turn over. Instead, inexplicably, it leapt. Snarling, wolfish, its clawed fingers ripped at the guard's thighs as he attempted to step back. It clung, tearing at the flesh of the leg as other men stood enthralled, stuck between horror and hilarity. Two more guards edged tentatively forward, a combination of wooden poles and over-confident hands pulling at the small being that continued to scratch and lash out. Panic crept in amongst the surrounding men, seemingly incapable of action.

"Get this thing off my le—" Its teeth sunk into the man's skin, piercing, drawing blood. "Get it OFF ME! GET IT OFF ME!"

Rough hands threw the feral boy-beast back to the

hard floor. Spears, point armed, slammed down to the stone at their feet, but the now fully alert creature twisted, contorted, avoiding the sharp points. In the commotion a heavy set guardsman stumbled, tripping over a wooden staff that rebounded off the hard ground. He fell forward, planting a hand on the slimy floor to stop his full bulk crashing down. The collective pause was enough. The wild child set itself on its haunches. Its eyes flamed with lupine savagery.

With a growl that belied its infantile age, the power and violence with which it landed on the man's arm and shoulder brought shouts and cries of dread. Tearing at the man's tunic, the swipes of its nails drew blood. The heavy man collapsed to the stone, thrashing in pain. Clambering higher on his body, the beast sunk its teeth into the guard's cheek. The scream echoed all round, freezing his colleagues who watched on in terrified disgust. The child did not let go. With its mouth full of fatty flesh it wrenched its head back, ripping away muscle and tissue from the bone in a bloody display of power and ferocity. Mouths gaped, aghast. The creature reared up again from its perch atop its prostrate prey, looking around at the disturbed and dumbstruck audience, crimson-stained chin and chest, its face the embodiment of utter rage. Finally, it sensed its chance and hurtled away down the corridor, hands like paws on the ground, rounding the curve and away, trailing spots of red in its wake.

No one saw the tiny figure appear again at the top of the sunken staircase between the castle walls, looking ever round, searching for the shadows. No one saw it manoeuvre its way through narrow windows and gaps, like a cat, leaving the castle behind, ridding its memory of the corridors and chaos. No one saw it slide between the houses of the people sleeping contentedly, stealthily and purposefully finding the paths out of Fenwood, out of civilisation, out of existence. The great protective arms of the trees welcomed him and closed behind him. He was one of them. Of them.

*   *   *

The Queen could not sleep. She lay awake in the darkness, soft covers pulled up almost over her head to ward off distractions from sleep, but her mind would not settle. Thus it was that she heard the faint rattle of the door handle turning and the patter of small feet on polished flagstone. To begin with she did not turn as a tiny body clambered onto the bed and burrowed under feathered covers.

"Mummy…" The whispered voice brought a regal smile to the older lady's lips. "Mummy? Are you sleeping?" Shuffling round to face her daughter, the Queen could not help but giggle at the delight in the little girl's face.

"Yes, darling, I'm sound asleep," she joked, bringing a stifled shriek of joy from the princess.

"I'm not sleepy, Mummy." The girl's dainty fingers touched her mother's nose and lips.

"Me neither, sweetheart." She kissed the fingertip that touched her bottom lip. "Have you had a bad dream?"

"No, Mama, I have not even been to sleep."

"Oh dear me." The Queen looked adoringly at the innocent face beneath the covers beside her. "Shall we see what the moon has to show us?"

The night breeze blew wisps of their hair from their faces. Ivy's hands held steadily on to the rough, stone balcony. Behind her, her mother laid a comforting and precautionary hand on her daughter's back. Neither spoke, content to stand in each other's company. Out over the rolling roofs of Fenwood, the moon illuminated the last curls of smoke as it drifted out across the fields and down the valley. As it gathered over the treetops of the forest, an ethereal mystery emanated out across the land, glowing in the power of the moon. The Queen allowed a private exhale of relief slide out into the night air. A city of calm. A world at peace. A Queen empowered to rule. A mother free to love. After such chaos and violence of the recent past, she drew strength from the earth beneath her feet, from the child that stood by her side, and from the woman who had changed the course of their lives.

A sound below them broke her train of thought. A shadow stretched in the flickering glow of the torches that hung on the outer walls. A huddled creature scurried on all fours toward the safety of the township.

"Mummy, do you see…?" She pointed, but the girl's voice faded as the cowering form melted into the shadows. The Queen, brow furrowed, looked down at her daughter.

"Was that some kind of animal, Ivy?"

The child only shrugged in response. They both watched intently for some moments in case the beast returned. Looking quizzically at each other, they gave up their watch and turned to head into the chamber within. Ushering her daughter back inside, the Queen gave one last glance out across the land. Standing on the edge of the shadows, near where the creature had dissolved into the night, a lone wolf stood and gazed into the darkness. It appeared calm, watchful, eyes piercing the gloom. High above, the silver-haired lady looked on, wondering if it had anything to do with the figure that had run from the cover of the castle. Then, without noticing a turn of the animal's head, yellow eyes were on her. And yet the Queen felt no fear. She had the sense that the wolf knew who she was, understood her. A feeling that she had sensed before passed between them. Maintaining eye contact, the wolf lowered its head, almost in a semi-bow, the Queen thought, before offering a low growl to the night. With a final glance up at the lady above, the wolf headed in the direction of Fenwood town, and ultimately, the forest.

*   *   *

The Histories tell of an 'immaculate conception'; a
Queen giving birth to a child of the land, so desperately
wanted that the Gods blessed her with motherhood.
The castle locked its secrets deep behind reinforced
solid oak doors, just as the forest covered its mysteries
with boughs and undergrowth. The King became a
footnote in a dusty volume on a shelf. Tolva lived
longer in memory; her legacy roaming free on the valley
sides above the town. The people of Fenwood remained
contentedly oblivious to the events that had shaped and
destroyed lives. They went about their work, toiling with
appreciation by day; by night the moon shone with a
mischievous threat of turmoil, but Fenwood slumbered
in peace. The breeze whispered its secrets and danced
with the leaves of the forest.

Somewhere, a wolf howled.

The whispering wind carried the words of change, of new life. It's soothing voice of challenge turned leaves and ran along branches, penetrating the cracks and voids that time and weather had shaped. It trickled along streams, rippled through grasses and tumbled down hills, reaching further, deeper into the forest, awakening old bastions of a bygone time.

At last, as the faintest of murmurs, the words found their way to the ancient waters of the silent pool, piercing the protective wooded shield and congregating at the banks of the dormant force. The old willow dipped its melancholy arms to the still, fallow waters.

"Awaken, brother. It is time."

ABOUT THE AUTHOR

Richard has lived in Portishead with his family for 10 years, moving to the Bristol area from London. He has been a secondary school English teacher for 20 years since completing his teacher training after graduating with a degree in English, Film and Drama from Reading University. A keen film fanatic and sports fan, Richard enjoys adventuring with his family and, when at home, writing. 'Wolf Mother' is his second novel after the success of 'The Pool', seeing him return to the land of Fenwood to explore further the themes of loyalty, chaos and nature.

Instagram – rich_collis_author

Facebook – Richard Collis